Books in the Antique Shop Mysteries series

The Christmas Riddle

Susan Sleeman

Annie's®
AnniesFiction.com

Library of Congress-in-Publication Data
The Christmas Riddle / by Susan Sleeman
p. cm.
I. Title
     2016934155

CountrySamplerFiction.com
(800) 282-6643
Antique Shop Mysteries™
Series Creator: Shari Lohner
Series Editor: Shari Lohner
Cover Illustrator: Bonnie Leick

10 11 12 13 14 | Printed in China | 9 8 7 6 5 4 3

"This is bad." Maggie Watson pulled up to the crumbling two-story house and glanced at her friend June McGillis. "You didn't mention the place was falling down."

"That's because I didn't know." June stared up at the eighteenth-century Georgian house and a deep frown drew down her usual cheerful smile. Even then, the short cut of her strawberry-blond hair gave her an impish look.

Maggie shifted into park but left her car idling. The windshield wipers swished away the heavy snow that had been falling for the last three hours. From what she'd been told, this weather wasn't unusual for December in Somerset Harbor. She'd only recently moved to town after inheriting Carriage House Antiques and Sedgwick Manor from her Aunt Evelyn.

Maggie had always dreamed of owning an antiques shop. As a widow whose college-age daughter had recently left the nest, it was the perfect time for a new adventure. So Maggie had relocated to Somerset Harbor to run her late aunt's estate and learn the antiques business alongside June, who served as the shop's manager.

June clicked her tongue. "I'd heard that Adele Kessler let the place go, but this is a travesty. Such an amazing old piece of architecture. It survived for almost three hundred years, and now it's falling apart." She shook her head sadly.

The house sat in a wide clearing at the end of a secluded driveway lined with tall trees, their limbs bare and waving in the wind. Between wiper swipes, Maggie caught glimpses of chipped peach paint with gray clapboards peeking through.

The porch sagged as if melting into the fresh blanket of snow covering the landscaping.

Maggie was heartsick at seeing the historic property in such a state of disrepair. "What happened, do you think?"

"No one knows for sure. Her son, Chad, who lives near here in Portland, claims she became too frail to leave home, and he hired a live-in nurse. Apparently, she wouldn't let workers onto the property to maintain the place. Or anyone else for that matter. She even declined visits from Pastor David."

"Sounds like you don't believe the story."

"I'm not sure what to believe. All I know is Adele was heavily involved at Old Faith Chapel until five years or so ago. Then everyone stopped hearing from her, and she died suddenly a few weeks ago."

"Perhaps she had a stroke. That would be sudden."

"Maybe. It's all very odd to me. A little disturbing too, I guess."

Maggie patted June's arm. "You should have said something before this. You could have stayed back at the shop."

"Are you kidding?" June's sullen expression suddenly disappeared and her love of antiques lit her face. "Adele had an amazing antiques collection, most of it going back to her ancestors who came over from England. I've got a good feeling that we're going to be adding some gems to our inventory today."

June, who was five years older than Maggie, not only managed the shop but had become a trusted friend as well. She could always brighten any situation, and her sensible nature was invaluable.

"You ready to do this?" she asked.

"Am I ever." Maggie climbed out into the snow.

An eddy of cold wind whipped snow into her face. She tugged up her coat collar and put her head down. She might have lived in the Northeast all her life, but at forty-four years old, she could safely say that she grew less tolerant of winter with every passing year.

They waded through waves of knee-high snow to the porch steps, following the footprints of others who were at the house for the estate sale. Wood rot damaged the columns so that they listed precariously to the side. The boards groaned and creaked as the women approached the paneled front door, where they were pleasantly surprised to find its decorative crown in good shape.

Inside, they paused to stomp the snow from their boots on a wide rug in the expansive foyer. Crumbling plaster exposed wooden laths on the high ceilings and faded walls. A once-magnificent mahogany banister led up to a second-story landing, and tattered floral carpet on the stairs tarnished the potential beauty of the space.

"It's not much better in here." Maggie whispered to keep her voice from carrying across the foyer to the estate sale employee sitting at a folding table. Suddenly, a thought struck her. "What if this place fell apart not because Adele didn't want people on her property, but because she was broke? It could mean she sold the quality antiques long ago to try to keep this place going."

"Let's hope not."

Maggie peeked into the adjoining rooms. Tables filled with items lined the middle and large furniture pieces sat along walls. From her location, it was hard to determine the quality of the items on sale. It didn't help that the people who picked over the tables hid many things from view.

"Ready to get in there?" June gestured to the crowded room.

"Yeah, let's get to it." Maggie took one last look up, silently praying that the ceiling wouldn't fall down around them, and then stepped into the dining room.

Maggie had attended crowded sales in the past, so she was right at home squeezing into small gaps to peruse the items covering every square inch of the long tables. It didn't take her long to determine that the furniture was reproduction and the tables held basic household items. She reached the end before June and continued into the parlor. She was pleased to see that she was the first person to enter the room, and her focus traveled straight to a red mercury glass vase filled with a rather hideous old flower arrangement.

"Yes!" she whispered and rushed to it. She carefully lifted the vase to check the bottom for a maker's mark.

June appeared at her side. "That looks real."

The only thing Maggie knew about mercury vases was that they could be valuable. "How can you tell?"

June pointed to the raised dots around the bottom of the twenty-inch-tall vase. "See how it's decorated with enamel work? That tells me it's authentic Bohemian mercury glass from the 1880s. The intricate hand painting against the satin matte finish is also a telltale sign."

Maggie eyed the vase. "You're sure it's authentic?"

"Positive."

"Then it was worth battling the snowstorm to get out here." Maggie settled the vase in the crook of her arm and peeked around the tattered flowers at June. "I'm glad this was included with the household items. They probably didn't even think about having an expert look at it to see if it had value."

June plucked at one of the fake flowers and a cloud of dust filtered into the air. "My guess is someone took one look at this horrid arrangement and assumed the vase was also worthless."

"I'll replace these with a Christmas arrangement and the vase will be perfect for the Candlelight Home Tour." The historical society was decorating Hayward Mansion for Christmas to raise funds and to give the people of Somerset Harbor a holiday treat at a truly magnificent old home.

"Bring the vase to our meeting tonight. Everyone will be excited to see it."

Chatter drew Maggie's attention toward shoppers filtering into the room. Many of them paused to evaluate the vase with keen eyes. "Let's get through the rest of the things before the crowd gets pushy."

They traveled down the tables, and then wandered past the furniture. Maggie spotted nothing else of value, though she was amused to see a man snatch an early '80s food dehydrator as if he'd found gold.

As the estate sale employee rang up the vase, Maggie nodded at the high arched openings above the doorways and leaned close to June. "This place may be falling down, but it's still fun to see the inside of an old Georgian home."

June stared into the distance, her expression dreamy. "I'd love to get a look at the upstairs."

"I saw a guy who looked like he might be the estate curator in the other room. Why don't I go talk to him while you finish up here?"

"Sounds good."

Maggie worked her way through the shoppers toward a man who made her think of Ichabod Crane. He stood in the dining room, eyeing the shoppers down a long nose that reminded her of a snipe's beak. As Maggie approached, his glassy-green eyes came to life, and he stood at attention, towering over her.

"May I help you?" he asked, his East Coast accent thick and heavy.

"I'm Maggie Watson. I own Carriage House Antiques in Somerset Harbor."

A hint of a smile lifted the corner of his mouth. "I knew your aunt Evelyn. What can I do for you?"

"I was wondering if my friend and I could take a quick tour of the house."

He shook his head hard, a scrap of black hair in the center

of his scalp whipping about wildly. "No one is allowed beyond the rooms designated for the sale."

"But—"

"I'm sorry," he interrupted. "Those are my instructions from the executor of Adele's estate. I cannot make any exceptions."

June joined them, the vase tucked safely under her arm. "I know Adele's son, Chad. Perhaps you can contact him and ask if we can view the home."

"Chad?" The curator flashed a momentary expression of confusion before he controlled it. "I don't know what you two are trying to pull here. Adele had no children." He glared at them. "Let me show you to the door."

He shooed them to the entrance and opened the door, but Maggie planted her feet on the wide plank floor. She wasn't about to be thrown out of an estate sale. A flurry of snow whipped into the foyer, and shoppers waiting to pay gave them nasty looks for letting in the cold.

The estate curator gestured more forcibly at the door. "Ladies."

"C'mon," June whispered. "We should go before he gets a bouncer." She shot a pointed glance at a large man who seemed bored as his wife meticulously picked through items on the table.

Maggie stifled a giggle and walked through the doorway with June behind her.

"That was strange." June handed the vase to Maggie and tugged together the lapels of her bright red coat. "Everyone in town knows Adele had a son. Why wouldn't the curator know that?"

"Why indeed?" Maggie groaned as she bent to settle the vase on the floor in the back of her car. "I didn't notice before how heavy this vase is." She carefully wrapped it in the worn quilts she kept to protect her finds. She thought about pulling out the flowers to look inside, but hastily removing the wire stems could scratch the interior. She would have to be patient until she got back to the shop and could take her time.

"Everything's a little off at this place," June huffed as she got into the car.

Maggie faced the house again. A vortex of snow swirled in the air and obscured the lines of the building. A feeling of desolation settled into Maggie's heart and a shiver claimed her body.

"I agree. Something's not right here," she said as she opened her car door. "Not right at all."

2

Maggie clutched the new vase to her side as she hurried down the sidewalk toward Hayward Mansion, June beside her. Their boots crunched through snow that had developed a crusty surface throughout the day.

Maggie was as eager to get out of the cold as she was to get a glimpse inside the mansion. She'd only been in Somerset Harbor for a few months, and she'd passed the house many times but hadn't gotten a chance to tour it. The mansion hadn't been open for tours, as the Hayward family occupied the home in the warmer months. However, they wintered in Florida, and this year, they had volunteered to let the historical society host tours during the annual Candlelight Home Tour.

"It's going to be a huge challenge to pull off our project in such a short time." Maggie's teeth chattered as she spoke.

"If anyone can get the mansion decorated in time for the tour, we can." June's cheeks were red from the cold and her excitement.

Maggie agreed as they rounded the corner to the two-story Federal-style mansion. She had been welcomed by the amazing women of the historical society and had come to consider them some of the most thoughtful, industrious people she'd ever known. She felt grateful to have been so warmly embraced by the group. She never would have imagined this life three years ago when her beloved husband, Richard, passed away. Yet here she was in a new town, with a new home and a new group of friends. They certainly made it worth enduring Maine in the winter.

A biting wind stole Maggie's breath, and she thought about lowering her head to stay warmer, but she didn't want to miss getting a good look at the mansion. The pristine white home featured stately columns and a matching picket fence surrounding the large yard. With the exterior lights glowing warmly in the dark night, she could easily imagine the people who'd lived in the well-kept home since the early 1800s. *How different this place is from Adele's run-down Georgian manor.*

They climbed the steps and kicked the snow from their boots under the small covered porch before moving into the warm foyer. Maggie balanced the vase and shed her coat as she admired a winding wood banister curling up wide stairs. Chatter from other members of the Somerset Harbor Historical Society drifted from the parlor.

"Sounds like we're the last ones to arrive." Maggie hung her coat on a wooden coat tree next to June's.

The parlor boasted robin's-egg velvet curtains with matching chairs and sofa. The other historical society members sat near a tall balsam fir they would soon cover in period-specific decorations.

"What in the world is that monstrosity?" Ruth Harper ran a hand through her short gray hair, eyebrows arched as she stared at Maggie's vase. Peering over her glasses, she certainly looked the part of the society's president.

Fellow members Fran Vosburg, Liz Young, Daisy Carter, and Ina Linton stopped talking and stared up at Maggie from the sofa and plump chairs.

"This?" Maggie feigned innocence and held out the gaudy arrangement. "It's a lovely decoration I bought at an estate sale today. I thought it would be perfect in the foyer for the Candlelight Home Tour. Don't you all agree?"

"But . . ." Ruth's words fell off, and she gaped at the arrangement.

Daisy, whose personality was as big as her teased hair, raised a suspicious eyebrow at Maggie. "And you usually have such good taste."

"That thing is ugly." Ina spoke in her usual forthright tone.

Maggie and June broke out laughing.

"Oh, this is a joke? Thank goodness," Ruth said with a sigh of relief.

"Don't worry. I'll replace this arrangement with something tasteful for Christmas," Maggie promised, still chuckling.

"The vase is authentic Bohemian mercury glass from the 1880s," June said excitedly.

Ruth examined Maggie's find. "It's a lovely vase."

"I think so too." Maggie set it on the coffee table for everyone to admire.

Ruth resumed her seat, picked up her clipboard, and pulled out a pen tucked behind her ear. She focused on Maggie and June as she lifted her coffee cup. "We've already helped ourselves to the refreshments. Why don't you grab a snack in the dining room and we'll get started?"

She pointed to a large cased opening at the end of the room. Maggie and June passed under the archway and found Daisy's artful spread on the Federal inlaid cherry sideboard. As the owner of The Busy Bean coffeehouse, Daisy provided refreshments for the meetings, and Maggie was more than happy to sample her delicacies.

Maggie plated a raspberry scone and poured hot water into a cup for chamomile tea. June also chose Daisy's pastry of the day drizzled with white icing, but she paired it with black coffee. They carried their food back to the living room.

"Once we've finished eating, we'll take a quick tour of the house," Ruth announced. "I'm hoping that each of you will take on the responsibility for decorating a room on the first floor. As we tour, you can shout out when you see a room you want to take charge of. Maggie, I suppose since you have that fabulous vase already, you'd like to take the foyer so you can showcase it."

Maggie swallowed a bite of pastry. "If no one minds."

Nods and murmurs of agreement traveled around the room.

"I'll put you down for the foyer." Ruth jotted a note on her pad.

Fran sat forward. "If we're calling dibs, I want to do this room. I love all the rich fabrics in here." This was no surprise. At thirty-six, Fran was the youngest member of the society, and she owned The Quilt Cupboard, where she sold beautiful quilts and fabrics.

Ruth made another note on her pad and gave Fran a smile. "I knew you'd like this room."

Ina stood and stared up at the fir. "How are we ever going to decorate such a massive tree? It's going to take boxes and boxes of ornaments. Do we even have that many?"

"I've done some research on tree decorations from the 1800s," Ruth said. "You might be surprised to learn that many of them were of the handmade-craft variety. Instructions were included in popular magazines at the time, and I've located several patterns for us to use in making them. They're not hard, but they'll take time to make." Ruth tapped her clipboard. "I've brought instructions for some paper streamers tonight."

"Sounds like something even I could make." Daisy chuckled.

"I thought so," Ruth said. "If everyone pitches in, we can add them and some other decorations to the nice assortment of glass ornaments we've collected over the years. They also used fruit and nuts on their trees in the early 1800s. We'll have to wait to decorate with those until the day before the tour."

"I can only make a few decorations," Daisy stated. "With Christmas just around the corner, I'm up to my eyeballs in baking. And this year I'm packaging and selling my special coffee blends."

Maggie had to admit that Daisy, though usually enthusiastic and bubbly, did look like she might want to curl up on the plush sofa, light a roaring fire in the large stone fireplace, and snuggle in for a long nap instead of planning ways to decorate the home.

"June," Maggie said, "if we team up, we could keep the supplies at the shop and work on decorations throughout the day."

"Sure." June's wide smile crinkled her eyes.

"Okay, it's settled." Ruth clapped her hands. "We'll each contribute as many decorations as we can. I'd like to meet every night for a few minutes to check our progress. We can gather here and hang the ornaments. Does that work for everyone?"

"Agreed," Ina said. "Now let's work off some of these sweets by taking that tour."

"Follow me." Ruth tucked her clipboard under her arm and led the group out of the parlor. In the billiard room were heavy wood paneling and ornately carved furniture from the 1800s. Louis XVI chairs upholstered in the same blue velvet that shone in the parlor sat around a large tufted ottoman and were anchored with a blue-and-black braided rug, which sported four conspicuous indents.

"Oh good," Ruth said. "Usually there's a big billiard table on the rug and a big-screen TV on that wall, but it looks like the Haywards moved them as I asked. I didn't know how we were going to make those period appropriate."

"I'll take this room," Daisy said. "It's small, and I can handle that with my crazy workload."

Ruth noted it and the tour continued. Her boots clicked on the original heart pine floor as she marched purposefully into the library, with its subtle burgundy velvet drapes and an ornately carved French horsehair sofa with a wool covering that matched the drapes. The plaster walls were a cream color and thick crown molding ran along the twelve-foot ceilings, painted a pristine white. The walls were lined with rich mahogany bookshelves full of beautiful hardcover books.

"This room is perfect for me." Liz Young, never greedy or hasty, claimed the room after waiting a beat. "One of my nativity sets will fit nicely on that table." She pointed at a round mahogany marble-topped table in the corner.

Ruth bobbed her head and noted it on her clipboard before moving on to the dining room. Eight plush red chairs circled a solid oak table in the middle of the room. Flowers and leaves were embroidered on the table skirt. Maggie paused to run her fingers over them, imagining generations of people dressed in their formal attire as they gathered for a meal.

"Now this is right up my alley." June joined Maggie. "We have the perfect china at the shop for this table. If you'll authorize me to use the dishes, that is, Maggie."

"Sure, as long as we keep an inventory. In fact, if you all want to stop at the shop or Sedgwick Manor to pick out items to borrow for the tour, I'd be glad to offer them to the cause."

"Perfect," Ruth said. "We can place a little card by the items stating they are on loan from the shop and drum up some business for you." She pressed on to the next room, which turned out to be the kitchen.

"Now if no one objects, I'd like to do the kitchen." Ruth searched their faces. "The job of coordinating the project will take up most of my time, so I'd appreciate an easier room to do."

"I'll do the kitchen." Ina put her hands on her hips. "I think coordinating this big project is plenty of work for you."

The women voiced their agreement.

"Thank you," Ruth said. "I'll put you down for the kitchen, Ina."

"What about the outside?" Liz asked.

"Let's get our husbands and a few men in town to help with

that," Ruth said. "We'll create a plan and provide the decor for them, and they can hang it."

"I know David will want to help, but his time is limited during the holidays," Liz said.

Maggie couldn't begin to imagine how much Pastor David must work during the Christmas season.

"Any time he can give would be appreciated." Ruth tucked her pen behind her ear. "Okay, that's all I have for tonight. I'll pass out ornament patterns and you can spend some time in your rooms formulating a plan before we clean up our refreshments."

"And by cleaning them up, I'm sure you mean finish eating them." Fran winked.

"Naturally." Ruth grinned. "We'll meet again tomorrow night to review our plans. Any questions?"

"Can we actually get all of this done?" Ina asked.

The usually cheerful, upbeat group muttered a bit.

"Sure we can," June said staunchly.

"And we can help each other," Fran added. "It'll be fun."

"All we need is a plan." Maggie pulled out the trusty notepad that she always had with her. "Let's get cracking."

Each disappeared to her own space with renewed spirits.

Maggie stood in the foyer and mulled it over in depth. Muted toile wallpaper with a cream-colored background covered the upper walls and oak wainscoting lined the walls. Maggie knew the perfect oak hall table from Sedgwick Manor to show off the vase. She'd have to buy the items for the arrangement, but she envisioned bright red poinsettia branches with pine boughs and cones. She jotted down a few notes and then joined the other women back in the parlor, where the energy was high.

They enjoyed their refreshments while chatting, but Maggie's gaze kept drifting to the vase. *Why is that vase so heavy? And what has been going on at the Kessler house?* She wanted to share the story of their afternoon. But the house was so disappointing and everyone was in such good spirits, she didn't have the heart to bring it up and ruin the Christmas cheer. *This one I will keep to myself.*

After they cleaned up and set a time to meet the next day, Maggie and June departed for Carriage House Antiques. It was like being in a New England winter wonderland when they stepped inside the shop. They were immediately greeted by a sleigh with carved Santas, steel runner sleds, wooden reindeer, and a feather tree covered in antique ornaments.

Maggie loved crossing the hardwood floors, walking under rustic chandeliers and among the festively decorated vignettes. Her favorites held charming country cottage decor and now boasted rustic holiday decorations as well. Strolling through the room made her feel closer to her aunt. But tonight, with the shop closed and the vase in her possession reminding her of the unsettled feeling from the Kessler home, she wanted to lock up and take the winding path to Sedgwick Manor to snuggle in with her cat, Snickers.

June pulled off her coat and led the way toward the workroom in the back. "You really are hoping there's some sort of mystery connected to this vase, aren't you?"

Maggie blinked in feigned surprise. "I have no idea what you're talking about."

"Oh, of course you don't." June smiled. She was beginning to know her friend well. "You don't need to get involved in another mystery, Maggie. Emily will be home for the holidays soon, and you'll want to spend time with her. Plus we've got far too much to do on the Hayward Mansion these next two weeks for you to get distracted."

Thinking of her precious daughter coming home from her first semester at Saint Joseph's College made Maggie's heart trip with joy. It wasn't easy adjusting to an empty nest. How she missed her sweet girl! "You know I'll make time for Emily, but . . ."

"Your sixth sense tells you something's wrong at the Kessler house and you won't be dissuaded."

"Exactly."

"Well then let's check it out." June opened the door to the workshop. "Clear out that vase, and we'll see if your intuition is on target yet again."

3

Maggie sat on one of the more comfortable stools in the shop workroom. Antique pendant lights cast a steady glow over the worn worktable.

She took a long breath, enjoying the scent of cedar oil that permeated the room as she loosened the fake greenery and carefully withdrew the tattered dried and silk flowers from the vase. Dust flitted through the air, and she fought back a sneeze when the arrangement came free from the vase. It was wrapped in heavy paper. She laid it on the counter, and then pressed out the crinkled, yellowed paper, which was missing a jagged corner.

June pointed at the base where flower stems were pressed into a round arrangement tool called a frog. "That metal frog might account for the weight."

"I suppose." Maggie peered into the vase and even tipped it upside down. "Nothing in here."

"Maybe your instinct was off this time."

"Maybe." Slightly disappointed, Maggie picked up the arrangement to dispose of it. Something metal fell from the flower stems and clanked onto the table.

"A key!" June exclaimed.

The object was indeed an old-fashioned key made of a silver metal. The heart-shaped top was covered in intricate scrollwork and two large jewels sparkled from the swirls. A small metal compass was affixed to the surface.

"Looks antique," Maggie said.

June leaned closer. "Sure does."

Maggie traced her finger around the top of the heart with its blood-red ruby and pine-green emerald. She picked it up and examined it from every angle. "I wonder if the heart shape holds any significance."

"Better yet," June said, "if those jewels are real, it has to be worth a good chunk of change."

Maggie nodded, her gaze riveted on the key. "I'll say."

"But why would anyone hide something so expensive in a dusty old arrangement?"

"Good question. Perhaps there's another clue in this mess." Maggie set the key on the counter. To take a better look at the arrangement, she began separating the flowers from each other. "Ah-ha!"

"What?" June asked.

"A note!" She pulled the missing piece torn from the floral wrapping from the base of the arrangement.

"What does it say?" June asked breathlessly.

Maggie laid it on the table, and they read:

> *Help! I don't know what the key opens. He thinks I do but won't tell because I want the money all to myself. He said he loved me, but it's the money he loves. Please help. He'll kill me if we don't find what it opens. He's coming. Hurry!*

Shocked, Maggie and June gawked at each other.

The sense of danger Maggie had briefly suppressed returned full force. "Do you think someone is actually in trouble, or is this note old?"

June picked up the note and held it by one corner. "The paper looks old, but that doesn't mean the note is. Someone could have torn it off at any time."

"But who?"

"I'm guessing that key is literally our key to finding out."

Maggie picked up the key and studied each intricate curve. "I agree that the key itself is old, but it looks like the compass was added later."

"In any case, we can't take any chances with the note, right?" June paused and nibbled on her lower lip. "We should call the police."

Maggie checked her watch and grabbed the phone. "They're not going to be happy to come out this late at night."

She was right.

Officer Robert Linton arrived, a frown on his boyish freckled face, and a notebook and pen in his hand. Maggie considered him a friend and wished she hadn't needed to bother him. He shook off his frown as he removed his cap, revealing close-cropped hair.

"Show me the vase and key first." His demeanor was pleasant yet professional, as she'd come to expect from a Somerset Harbor police officer, especially the usually cheerful Robert.

Officer Linton took his job seriously and was about Maggie's age, so she knew he had enough experience to handle her call.

She described the situation, trying to keep it short so she didn't waste his time.

He studied the key. "Can't say I've ever seen such a fancy key. Or one with a compass on it."

"I found that a bit abnormal too," June said.

"I'm not even sure it's a real key," Maggie added.

"You mean the jewels?" the officer asked.

"Those too, but what I meant is that it doesn't look like a key that's been used on a regular basis. More of a decorative piece, I think."

He took out his phone to snap pictures. "What about the vase?"

June provided him with a detailed description. He started

jotting notes, but it wasn't long before his eyes glazed over at the technical information June offered.

"It's a valuable piece," Maggie cut in, interrupting June with an apologetic look. "Not something that should have been grouped with cheap reproductions at the sale."

He closed his notebook. "Seems like either someone wanted the vase sold quickly so the key would be found, or the people in charge of the sale didn't know the true value of the vase."

"I hadn't even considered that the vase might have been put in the sale on purpose." Maggie mulled over the new idea.

"Makes sense," June added.

"And this is the note." Officer Linton bent down and scrutinized it. "I suspect it's either old or a practical joke."

"A joke?" Maggie asked. "You really think so?"

"In my opinion, a person in trouble wouldn't have taken the time to write such a detailed note. Plus, I suspect in their haste, they would have scribbled. Imagine yourself in that situation. I'm sure your hands would be shaking and you'd be panicked."

For the first time, Maggie realized that the note's penmanship was flawless. "You could be right."

"My guess is someone simply thought it would be a hoot to stir up trouble, so at some point, they ripped off this piece of paper and wrote the note. I mean, the house is old. All kinds of people have had access to it over the years, and especially recently with the estate sale."

Maggie could concede such a thing, but she doubted Officer Linton's theory. *Why am I not buying this argument? Do I just want to find a mystery here?* She wanted to be careful about sounding overly dramatic, so she kept her thoughts to herself.

"But," he continued, watching her, "we can't be too careful. I'll stop by the Kessler home and check it out. Be advised that the house is in the county's jurisdiction, not ours, so my visit will have to be unofficial."

"Does that mean if you see something wrong, you can't do anything?" Maggie asked anxiously.

"I'll have to play it by ear. I'll go by the estate and see what I can find. I'll call you after I check this out."

"Should I also call the county sheriff's department to help?"

"If it becomes obvious that we need to involve them, I'll give them a call," Officer Linton reassured her.

"Okay. Please remember to call me," she reminded him. She knew she could trust Robert with this.

He gave her a firm nod. She escorted him to the door and closed it behind him, a scowl spreading over her face.

"This is such a strange situation," June said. "I'm glad Robert is going to look into it. It'll be fine, Maggie. Now stop glowering."

Maggie tried to relax her face . . . and her mind.

"And I think he was right about the compass." June tapped the key. "It's downright weird. I'm leaning toward your way of thinking that this key doesn't actually open anything."

"I'm not sure about that," Maggie said. "I said I thought it wasn't used on a regular basis. But it could certainly open something."

June slid back on the stool. "What could it open?"

"I don't know, but I aim to find out." Maggie grabbed her tote bag. She was ready to be home. Snickers would definitely have a lecture prepared about her late arrival. "I can't help but think someone's life might be at stake here, even if Officer Linton isn't as convinced."

"If there's one thing I've learned about you, it's that your instincts are usually right." June's mouth opened in a wide yawn.

Maggie had to fight back one of her own. "We should get going."

"I couldn't agree more." They slipped into their winter wear and headed outside.

Maggie waited for June to start her car and back out before hurrying along the path to Sedgwick Manor. The wind howled over the freshly fallen snow, whipping it into little snow whirlwinds. Snow settled into Maggie's boots as she occasionally plowed through thigh-high drifts, and the icy coldness sent a shiver over her body. In hindsight, she should have taken the street instead of the path, though it was a much longer route.

She reached the wood footbridge that spanned the small stream cutting through the property. Raised from the ground, the bridge was icy and treacherous. Maggie gripped the handrail to prevent a nasty fall. She'd never been so thankful to see the glowing lights peeking through frosty windows of the manor's sunroom. Stiff fingers made it hard to unlock the door, but Maggie got it open and escaped into the heated room.

"Snickers," she called out to her cat. "I'm home."

He didn't respond. No surprise there. Why get up from his favorite perch? He knew she'd look for him. She'd long ago resigned herself to the fact that people don't own cats; cats own their people.

She took off her coat, hat, and gloves and shook off the snow. Boots came off next and she put on the slippers she'd left by the heat register. Her cell phone rang and she shoved her frozen fingers into her bag to retrieve it.

"Maggie Watson," she answered on her way to her bedroom, making sure to take the bag that held the key. She wasn't about to let it out of her sight.

"Officer Linton, Ms. Watson. I stopped by the Kessler house and found no one home and the lights out. The place is buttoned up tight. I'm about to go off duty, but another officer will stop by in the morning to check too."

Snickers meowed from the bed, where he was curled up in Maggie's favorite quilt from her mother.

"You don't think this is a current note, then?"

"I'm not saying that. All I can tell you is that there doesn't appear to be anyone at the home. If there is domestic trouble over whatever that key opens, it's not happening there."

"But you didn't go inside, so how can we be sure?"

"I didn't see or hear anything that could justify gaining entry to check on a person's well-being, so I had to walk away. But I'll make a full report for the chief. If he wants to open an official case, we can proceed."

"You really couldn't find a way inside?" She ran her fingers through Snickers's soft coat of fur and sank down on her bed with its canework head- and footboards.

"I'm treading on thin ice here. If I forced my way into the home and found nothing wrong, the city would end up paying for any incurred damages, and the chief wouldn't be too happy with me. And again, the house is out of my jurisdiction, which makes it very complicated. If I broke in and nothing was amiss, the sheriff's department could even hold me responsible for a crime. I know this is important to you, but I have to follow protocol."

She didn't blame him, but someone needed to get a look inside that house. *Looks like it's up to me to make that happen.* How, she didn't know, but she had to find a way. Determined, she thanked Officer Linton and hung up.

"That didn't go as I'd hoped, Snickers." She scratched under his chin and received a throaty purr in response. "As much as I'd like to crawl into bed beside you, I have work to do."

One last ruffle of Snickers's ears and she made for the office at the front of the house. The small space always reminded her of Aunt Evelyn, especially the flame mahogany pedestal partner's desk. Aunt Evelyn had often completed her paperwork at the desk that was the centerpiece of the room. When Maggie would visit as a child, she would snuggle into the overstuffed chair next to it, content to be in the room with her aunt. And now, here she was, using the same desk for her own paperwork.

She ran her fingers over the embossed leather top and let out a nostalgic sigh. Then her laptop screen caught her attention and she remembered her purpose. She hoped to use her computer to discover additional details about the key and to locate experts who could date it and authenticate the jewels.

She laid the key next to her on the desk so she could compare it with any pictures she might discover. Snickers padded into the room and jumped onto her lap. She held him close with one arm, enjoying his warmth in the drafty old room as she searched through pictures of antique keys on the Internet.

An hour later, she'd located several pictures from the eighteenth century that were similar to the key, but none were as elaborate as the one she now possessed.

Maggie stretched from hunching over the computer and faced Snickers. "What do you think, Snickers? Do you think the key is as old as some of these pictures suggest? Of course, it might not even be authentic."

Snickers rolled onto his back and stretched, then curled into a tight ball. He covered his little pink nose with a paw to keep out the chill. She was ready to curl up too, but she had a few more things to do before she could sleep. She quickly searched for expert appraisers nearby and then jotted down their names and phone numbers so she could call them about the key first thing in the morning.

Satisfied that she'd made as much progress as she could for the night, she closed her computer. The wind howled outside, rattling the windows. She tugged her sweater tighter and stared at the key and note.

An ominous feeling emanated from the items, and her heart rate kicked up.

She tried to shake off the feeling as she gently wrapped the key in tissue paper from the drawer, but her mind wouldn't cooperate. *That note is urgent. Someone is in trouble.*

"Snickers, old pal," she muttered out loud, "exactly what kind of mess have I gotten myself into this time?"

4

The next morning Maggie called several appraisers, and then pushed back from the desk in Sedgwick Manor's office. Snickers meowed and rolled to his back on the tufted bench in front of the window. He stretched striped legs above his head, his snowy white chin shining in a warm beam of light filtering through the glass.

"What do you think the key is for, Snickers?" Maggie asked.

A purr rumbled from his chest as he rolled to his side and started licking his paws.

"Some help you are." She laughed and enjoyed the view overlooking the estate's front lawn mounded in snowdrifts.

She would have loved to sit back with another cup of coffee and light a fire in the restored fireplace with its intricate iron screen instead of going out in the bitter cold, but a woman's life could be hanging in the balance. Maggie had to proceed with her investigation without a moment's delay.

She zipped her jacket and caught sight of the names Nigel Holman and Erwin Arnett on her purple notepad. Nigel was a certified gemologist who specialized in antique jewels, and Erwin was an expert in antique locks. She'd emailed a picture of the key to each of them after she'd spoken to them. They were both so intrigued by the key that they'd agreed to see her in an hour at Nigel's jewelry store in Portland.

She tugged on her hat and checked the time on the heavy brass nautical clock sitting on the desk. When Maggie had been younger, she and her aunt would make up stories about seagoing vessels in early American history where the clock would have sat on the captain's desk. They would muse about what Captain Thomas Sedgwick, who had built the manor for his wife, had been like, and what adventures he might have had. Maggie often thought she'd gotten her love of history from those days spent with her aunt.

"Okay, Snickers, I need to go." She rubbed his tummy. "You be a good kitty and don't get into any trouble."

He replied with a long meow of contentment.

"You really have the life, you know that?" She patted his head. "I'll see you tonight."

She picked up her bag and made sure her key, the note, and her notepad were inside before she went out to the car. She was resolved to track down the key's purpose and learn if a woman truly was in danger. Not even the bright winter sun sparkling across the snow could distract her.

Once on the road, she was thankful that the road crews had already cleared the way, allowing her to arrive in Portland fifteen minutes ahead of her schedule. As she walked into the jewelry store, it took her eyes a moment to adjust. Though the shop was brightly lit, the artificial lighting didn't compare to the blinding white snow covering the landscape outside. Her gaze ran over tall wooden display cases that were likely from the early 1900s. Precious and semiprecious stones of every cut, color, and size twinkled at her from the cases. A large pegboard behind the counter held small tools, and an antique library card catalog sat below it. The sign outside noted that Nigel repaired jewelry, so Maggie suspected the catalog contained parts for his repair work.

A thin man with a bald head, thick glasses, and a graying goatee stood behind a display case. He wore a black corduroy vest topped with a paisley bow tie. Next to him stood a squat man with a full head of silvery hair, who was dressed in worn corduroy pants and an old fisherman's sweater.

"May I help you?" the thin man asked.

"I have an appointment with Mr. Nigel Holman."

"Maggie Watson, I presume." He beamed at his own Sherlock Holmes reference.

Maggie had heard this joke often, but it still amused her. "Yes."

He extended his hand. "I'm Nigel and this is Erwin Arnett. We've been dying to see the key in person since you sent the picture."

Maggie wished she thought it was so fascinating instead of worrying. "I appreciate you both agreeing to meet with me. Shall we get started?"

Nigel slid a black velvet tray across the counter. "You can put the key here."

Maggie placed her bag on the counter and carefully unwrapped the key. She settled it on the fabric, admiring how the jewels glistened against the dark background.

Erwin let out a low whistle. "It's even more spectacular than I thought. May I pick it up?"

"Please do."

He lifted it reverently from the velvet and turned it in all directions. He dug a magnet from his pocket and set it on the key, but it didn't stick. "Just as I suspected. The key is likely made of forged iron, which was very common in keys made before 1900." He hovered a magnifying glass over the key. "No maker's mark, which also means we're presumably looking at pre-nineteenth century."

"You think it was made in the 1700s or earlier?" Maggie clarified.

"Yes. And the design is simple, made before the lever tumbler lock was perfected in the late 1700s." He looked up. "In summary, you have an early-1700s key here. There's not much sign of wear, so I doubt it was used often, if at all."

"Now, the compass is anomalous," he continued, peering at the key again. "It's a newer addition soldered onto the iron.

I'm not sure who would want to deface such a lovely example of an early eighteenth-century piece."

"I thought it was peculiar too," Nigel weighed in.

"As do I," Maggie said. "Any idea what the key might be used for?"

"It's large enough for a door, but it might also fit a trunk or wardrobe. Honestly, though, if these jewels are real, I doubt it was used for any item that was regularly opened. Could even be a ceremonial key, symbolic of some achievement but not functional."

With the age of the key determined, Maggie was even more interested in it. She faced Nigel. "What about the jewels? Are they real?"

"Let's take a look." He picked up a loupe and put it to his eye, then took the key from Erwin. A few grunts and mumbles later, he strode to the end of the counter where a large microscope sat. He placed the key under the lens and bent over it. "A clean, pristine, and sharp-cut facet."

"It's real, then?" She held her breath.

He gave Maggie a patient look. "Perhaps you'd like to look around the shop while I finish my evaluation. Or you and Erwin could talk quietly."

Maggie took the hint. "What woman doesn't like to look at jewelry?" She made her way around the room, trying to focus on the exquisite pieces, but today she had no interest in the diamonds and other precious stones in the cases. She wanted to hover over Nigel as he worked, but he wasn't charging for the appraisal so it wouldn't do to annoy him. However, she did keep an eye on the clock on the wall, which was shaped like a large diamond ring.

Half an hour later, Nigel finally swung around, a broad smile on his face. "You have an authentic piece here, Maggie. The jewels are all genuine and the cuts are exceptional."

Her excitement flared as she raced back to the counter. "So it's a key from the 1700s with a recently added compass and real jewels." She thought of something else. "And the value? What's the key worth?"

"The key itself isn't all that valuable, especially with the compass addition," Erwin said.

"The value is in the jewels," Nigel added. "I'd say at auction, you could expect to receive $10,000 or more."

"Ten thousand dollars?" She goggled at him for a moment. "You're sure?"

He chuckled. "You, my dear, have got to start trusting me. I've been doing this for a long time."

"I'm sorry, but it's so much money."

"That it is," he replied in a casual tone, as if he appraised gems of this value often. "Would you like me to put you in touch with a reputable auction house?"

"No!" she exclaimed, a little too tersely.

He took a step back, startled.

She calmed her emotions and lowered her voice. "I'm much more interested in discovering what the key might have been used for."

"As I mentioned," Erwin said, "it has very little wear, so I doubt it was used often. I'd lean toward a trunk, as it would be used less frequently than a door or even a wardrobe."

"Unless it was a secret door," she said, her mind already going to the great mystery a secret door might hold. "Is there anything else you can tell me about the key?"

He picked it up and analyzed it again. "No . . . no, I think that's it. If you'll allow me to share the picture you emailed to us, I can do some research and ask my colleagues if they might have any additional thoughts."

"Great idea," Nigel said.

"Please feel free to share it. If you don't mind, that is. I don't want to impose."

"Ms. Watson, one is not imposing when one shares such a rare find. I consider it an honor to be able to evaluate the key and help you discover more about its history."

Maggie jotted her cell number on the back of two business cards and handed one to each man. "You can reach me here with any information you find."

Nigel pocketed the card. "I'll have to stop by your store someday and we can talk antiques."

"I'd like that." She thanked him and began to wrap the key in its tissue paper.

"Now that you know the value of the key, you'll want to take better care of it than that." He reached under the counter and came up holding a plastic bag with his store logo on the outside. "There's a professional storage bag and polishing cloth in here."

She carefully placed the key into the cloth bag as they watched her intently. She suspected they were equally intrigued by the mystery and perhaps a bit jealous that she was the one who had found it.

They wouldn't be jealous if she told them about the note and the fact that a life might be on the line.

5

Maggie decided to stop at The Busy Bean on the way home. She loved the older building with its large picture window frosted on the corners. The day after Thanksgiving, Daisy had teetered from a ladder to hang fresh wreaths with bright red bows above that window and string garland with glittering lights on the eaves. The shop's large logo was mounted above a yellow-and-white canopy, in direct contrast to the holiday decor. The café's name was written in black script with a bright yellow bee preparing to dive into a large cup of coffee. It reminded Maggie of Daisy's hair, which she often styled in a beehive.

The bell above the door tinkled as Maggie entered. James Bennett, town alderman and a good friend of Maggie's, had told her that The Busy Bean had once been decorated in a nautical theme like so many of the businesses in town. When Daisy had taken over, she'd changed the decor to fit her personality, with lemony yellow and turquoise tables, chairs, and floor.

A joyful refrain of *Deck the Halls* played in the background as a mixture of nutty fresh-ground coffee and the sugary sweet scent of melted chocolate sent Maggie's stomach growling. A quick look at a beehive-shaped clock told her it was lunchtime. The place was bustling as usual and she scanned the room to see if James might be there. She spotted him at her favorite table overlooking the ocean. He saw her and waved.

"Hi, Maggie!" Daisy hollered, making the other diners shift to look at her. "I'll be over to take your order in a sec."

James had swiveled from his conversation with Daisy's husband, Harry, a lobster fisherman with reddened skin beneath a black stocking cap. Harry often popped in to visit his wife. He greeted Maggie, then said to James, "I'd better go home and get started on my honey-do list." He trundled off in Daisy's direction, clearly hoping to catch his wife for a goodbye kiss.

"Afternoon, Maggie." James's slate-blue eyes sparkled at her, reminding her of the gems she'd seen in Nigel's shop. "You're just in time to join me for lunch."

"I don't mean to invite myself, but I am hungry."

"Then have a seat."

James pulled out a chair for Maggie and the scent of cinnamon met her nose. She'd often caught him popping small cinnamon candies in his mouth from a little box he kept in his coat pocket. Somehow, the old-fashioned quirk endeared him to her.

"Please join him." Daisy came up behind Maggie. "That way he'll quit flirting with my staff, and all the women in the room can quit swooning over the nonstick bachelor."

James gave Daisy a look of mock offense. "I don't flirt!"

"Hah!" Daisy filled his coffee cup. "And it never snows in Somerset Harbor either."

"I've never heard something so outrageous about myself." James gave her a cheeky smile.

Daisy shook her head, smirking with fuchsia lips. "Today's special is piping hot chili with my homemade onion bread."

Maggie took the chair James still held for her, and Daisy filled the mug in front of her with rich black coffee. She pulled a selection of creamer cups from her pocket and handed them to Maggie. "What can I get you to eat, hon?" she asked.

"You know I love your chili."

"Coming right up." She pivoted, and her sneakers squeaked on the bright yellow vinyl flooring. Daisy always said it was a beast to keep clean, but she loved the sunny color because it made her happy as she mopped.

"You like Daisy's chili that much, huh?" James asked.

Maggie added creamer to her coffee. "I do like it, but more importantly, it's ready and hot on the stove. I don't have time for a long stay."

"Sounds like you're up to something."

She pulled her bag into her lap. "I bought an antique vase at the Kessler estate sale and found this stuffed in the flower arrangement along with a note." She pulled out the key and showed it to him, trying to keep it hidden from the other diners.

"Whoa!" he exclaimed, more loudly than she would have liked. A couple of the other diners glanced at them. James scooted closer and lowered his voice. "Is that real?"

"According to a Portland gemologist and a locksmith who both specialize in antiques." She dropped her voice to a whisper. "They said it's from the early 1700s, and it's worth $10,000."

"Ten thousand!" he yelped. "You're kidding."

Now their fellow diners were openly staring at them.

"Very subtle. Thank you for understanding that I didn't want all of Somerset Harbor to know about this," she said, chuckling. She stowed the key before anyone caught sight of it and ignored the stares. A waitress appeared—Daisy was really swamped now—with a bowl of chili and a hunk of onion bread. Maggie thanked her, then faced James and lowered her voice again. "I'm hoping to talk to Adele's son, Chad. Do you know him?"

"We went to school together, so yes. I knew him pretty well before he left."

She stirred the creamer and her coffee swirled into a warm brown color. "What can you tell me about him?"

"Nothing about him as an adult. He left town right after high school, but when he lived here, he got into some trouble with the law. Oddly, he also regularly attended Old Faith Chapel with his mom. Man, did that set the tongues to wagging."

"What exactly did he do?" Maggie asked.

"Petty crimes. Stealing, underage drinking, that sort of thing. Nothing seriously bad." He rested his elbows on the table. "Most people didn't press charges. Guess they hoped he'd change his ways, or perhaps Adele convinced them not to, but each little incident drew a lot of gossip. He did end up doing a bit of community service, and I know he resented the people around here. I wasn't surprised when he took off and didn't come back."

"What about his dad?"

"He died when Chad was little." He shook his head. "We didn't see Adele in town often, but she was a church regular until she basically disappeared a few years ago. That whole thing was unusual."

"What do you mean?" Maggie took a sip of the coffee.

"One day out of the blue, Chad contacted Pastor David and told him that Adele wasn't ill but had become feeble. He said he'd hired a nurse to care for her, and she refused to see anyone. Even Pastor David."

"And they went along with it just like that?" Maggie asked.

"The nurse turned away everyone who attempted to visit, saying Adele refused to see them."

Maggie gripped her bowl for warmth, suddenly chilly in Daisy's cozy little café. "Do you know anything about the nurse?"

"No." He stared off into the distance and seemed lost in thought. "Man. I haven't thought about the Kessler family in years, but I have great memories of playing there as a kid."

"Do you know something about the history of the house, then?"

"Well, sure. It's been in their family since it was built in 1730 by a shipbuilder named Lewis Kessler. Chad and I used to pretend we were Lewis. Of course, what we really liked was playing pirates and digging for buried treasure. I always wanted to be the pirate." He gave her a grin, but it quickly faded. "One time we dug for treasure near the old cellar door, and in the process, we dug up one of Adele's prized heirloom roses. Boy, did we get in trouble."

Maggie could easily envision him as a child with a patch over his eye and a cardboard sword in his hand, digging for treasure with the same smile she'd seen a moment ago. "Did you stay friends after that?"

"Adele was so mad after the rose incident that I wasn't brave enough to go over again for several weeks." He sat back. "But I did eventually, and we stayed friends until Chad started getting into trouble."

"Has he ever come back for a visit?"

James rubbed his forehead. "I've never seen him or heard anyone else say they've seen him. The nurse was from out of town, so I bet he didn't even have to come back here to hire her."

"But what about food? I mean, Adele had to eat, right?"

"If she didn't want to have anything to do with the people around here, she probably sent the nurse somewhere else to shop. Or she had her food delivered."

Maggie swirled her coffee. "It's all puzzling to me."

"I agree, but there was something off about Adele ever since Chad left town. She never really recovered, I suppose. She used to hold big annual Christmas parties and invite the whole community. They were extravagant and a highlight of the holiday season around here, but they suddenly stopped too."

Maggie dug out her phone and showed James a picture of the vase. "Did you ever see this vase at the house?"

"I remember that from Christmas. Adele displayed it in the foyer."

"Only at Christmas?" she pressed.

"I never really noticed. As a kid I didn't care about antiques, and when I got involved in preserving old homes, I was more interested in the buildings than the furnishings."

"It would be a shame if Chad didn't come back to town and someone other than a Kessler got the house," Maggie observed.

"I doubt Chad will ever live here again. He has to know he wouldn't receive a warm welcome."

"Would it be too much to hope you have his address?"

"I don't, but I should be able to locate it if you think it will help."

"That would be great," she said earnestly. "I tried to go through the curator, but he claimed Adele didn't have any children. The thing is, there was nothing of value at the sale except the vase. I think the vase only got through because of the awful flowers."

"Well, I can assure you the house was once filled with antiques."

"So the big question is what happened to them?" Maggie frowned at her chili, which was getting cold.

"The valuable items are being sold at auction. I know the curator who handled the sale. He's well respected, so I doubt he's trying to pull a fast one on you. I can give him a call if you'd like."

"And can you question him about Chad?"

"Of course. Now tell me about this note."

She withdrew it from her bag. "It was torn from paper that was wrapped around the arrangement. The yellowing and the brittle texture make me think the paper is old, but I don't know about the ink."

James took his time contemplating it. "The ink seems fresher than you'd find on an old document."

"You think?"

He nodded. "We could send it off to be tested, but that would take time, and it doesn't sound like the writer has that. You called the police, right?"

"I did. Officer Linton checked it out."

"Then leave it to him."

"Why, James Bennett, if I didn't know any better I'd think you were worried about me." She winked at him to lighten the mood, but she received a concerned look instead.

"Tell me you'll let the police handle this." There was no humor in his tone.

"I'm sorry. Until I know if someone is in trouble, I can't promise anything."

"Just so you know," he said, meeting her eyes squarely, "I'm not about to stand by and let you get hurt. If you continue to look into this, I'll be keeping an eye on you."

She smiled, but she was thankful for his concern. *Who knows what I might find in this investigation? It could get dangerous.*

6

Maggie strode up to *The Somerset Harbor Herald*'s two-story building on the corner near the library. There was a fresh coat of white paint on the clapboard siding, and the navy blue shutters around the two large windows looked new. *This place looks better than I expected.* With news available 24/7 on the Internet, owner and editor Thad Jablonsky was struggling to make ends meet, and he couldn't afford the old building's upkeep. Then she noticed the small sign advertising Nate and Opal Gregory's respective landscaping and housekeeping businesses. They must've known Thad was in a tight spot, so they were keeping up his building in return for free advertising, which they didn't really need. Maggie smiled. The people in this town were so good to each other.

She opened the door, and the pungent odor of ink from the printing press hit her head-on. A tall rack to her right held a variety of newspapers, both national and local. On either side of the rack sat orange vinyl chairs from the sixties. Many residents often stopped by to read papers and chat with Thad.

Straight ahead was a worn wood counter covered with glass. A vintage wooden inbox sat atop the glass with a sign: Put Your News Here.

She approached the counter and found Thad seated at a dilapidated oak desk, tapping away at his computer. His shoulders were stooped under a plaid flannel shirt, and even from the side, she could see that his buzz-cut brown hair was well on its way to balding at the top.

"Hi, Thad."

He looked up and pulled off his reading glasses. "Well, Maggie. Come to place an ad?"

"Not this time. I'm trying to find information about Adele Kessler."

"Adele?" He stood and laid his ink-stained hands on the counter. "I sure was sorry to hear about her passing. Fine lady, she was."

Though Maggie hadn't known Adele, she nodded. "I bought a vase at her estate sale and was hoping you'd allow me to check your archives for information about it. I'd go to the library, but I did some research there last month and discovered their records on microfiche are spotty."

"Yeah, they started the project, and then decided not to waste the resources because I have a thorough archive in the old apartment upstairs." He tipped his head at the back of the room. "Door's in the back. The only thing I ask is that you make sure to put things back the way you found them."

"I won't make a mess," she promised.

"The archives go back to the newspaper's first edition. I can help you narrow down the time frame if you want."

"There might be one thing. James mentioned that the vase was used at Adele's famous Christmas parties. Do you know anything about the parties?"

"Sure do. There's no need to look at anything more current than December twenty-five years ago. Adele held her last party that year."

"Wow. Your memory is incredible if you can recall that."

"I should just take the compliment, but I have to be honest," he said, taking on a conspiratorial tone. "My son was born that year the night before Adele's party. I was looking forward to it as usual, but my son came first. So of course, we missed the party. Still, if I'd known it'd be the last one she'd ever throw, I might have gone for a few minutes."

"I wish I'd lived here at the time. You're the second person who's mentioned how amazing the events were."

"They were something, all right. First class all the way. I always did a big spread in the paper, so you'll at least be able to see pictures and read the write-up."

"Wonderful. Thank you again."

"Oh, no problem. Just let me know if you need any help." He went back to his computer.

She climbed the stairs to the second story. Inside, she shivered and pulled the zipper on her coat higher. Thad conserved money by not heating the space, and she could see her breath. She followed a short hallway to what must have been a living room when the upstairs had been an apartment. It was ringed with heavy metal shelves rising from floor to ceiling. A few rays of sun broke through dirty windows to shine on dingy yellow storage boxes, but it would take much stronger rays to make the place look inviting. The boxes were stacked in perfect lines, each dated on the end in bold black letters. She noted that individual boxes held a year's worth of newspapers.

There were framed articles and pictures on the walls, speaking to a happy past for Somerset Harbor. Occasionally, a retired governor, senator, and even—once—a former president had made his way through the town, and the *Herald* had been there every time. Maggie saw stories of construction of new buildings as well as tales of the community coming together to preserve old ones. *The more I learn about Somerset Harbor, the more proud I am of this place. I could browse this history all day. But that note . . .*

She had found Adele's obituary on the Internet and printed it off, and now she pulled it out of her tote. Maggie located the year Adele had been born. She'd start there and work her way to the year of the last party. She swiped away sticky cobwebs and heaved the box onto a table in the middle of the room, then brushed off a rickety chair. Dust took flight and danced in the sunlight as she flipped open the box. A musty scent contaminated the air as she dug carefully through crinkly pages to locate the month Adele had been born. She quickly perused the pages.

Footsteps sounded on the stairs. Maggie placed the newspaper back in the box and went to the door. Liz Young waved at her from the other end of the hallway. Maggie grinned. Liz would be of great help.

Liz's navy wool coat was topped with a fluffy white scarf tucked tightly under her chin. Her face shone with a sweet, trustworthy look that invited people to sit down with her and have a chat, which helped her in her work as a psychologist.

Maggie stepped back to let her in. "Liz, what are you doing here?"

Liz beamed at her. "I stopped by the shop to look at the antiques for my room in the Hayward Mansion. June told me all about the key and that you were here. I had a few hours to kill until my next group, so I thought I'd offer to help you dig through the papers."

Just like Liz.

"You are so sweet, and I'd love the company." Maggie started back toward the box she had abandoned. "But I warn you. It's frightfully cold in here."

"I guess we'll have to talk a lot to warm up the place." Liz peered around the room. "There's so much history here."

Maggie tapped the box. "I started the year Adele was born. So far I've found her birth announcement and also discovered that the Kesslers's annual Christmas party was a tradition even before she was born."

"I wonder if they had the same idea as you to use the vase as a Christmas decoration."

"James remembered seeing it at a party, and I've already found a mention of it in 1945." Maggie picked up the paper she'd dropped and spread it open in front of Liz. "It's described in the decorations mentioned in this article, but there aren't any pictures so I can't be positive it's the right vase."

"And of course, at some point, it was charged with holding the atrocious arrangement you bought."

Maggie smiled. "Don't remind me."

"Should we look at older papers to see if we can find out when the vase first showed up?"

"Great idea."

Liz carried an older box to the table. They sat side by side, chatting about local events and happenings as they flipped through dusty papers.

An hour later, Maggie sat back and flexed her fingers. "As a newcomer, it's fun to read about the town's history."

"I know what you mean." Liz pressed open a paper with a photo of Old Faith Chapel on the front page. "The church has barely changed, and this photo was taken nearly a hundred years ago."

"Too bad these archives don't go back to the 1700s when it was built."

"That would be amazing to see, wouldn't it? But at least much of the building is preserved for use today." Liz stared into the distance. "I can easily imagine the people coming to church back then. Heading down the two main aisles . . ."

"Climbing into the box pews," Maggie joined in. "Every Sunday when I pull the little door closed on the pew, I think of the people who might have sat in the very space I'm seated in."

Liz clutched Maggie's arm. "I'm so glad to hear that. I thought I was the only one who thought of it."

"When so much of the church's past is preserved in the building, it's easy to imagine, isn't it? The pulpit, the worn wood floors where faithful people have passed for hundreds of years." Maggie enjoyed the thought.

They both sat lost in a simpler time until Liz's phone rang and broke the spell.

She dug the phone from her pocket and frowned. "I need to take this. It's one of our members at church who's having a difficult time." She went out into the hallway.

Maggie didn't require a more detailed explanation. As a counselor, Liz often needed privacy and Maggie respected that. She started thumbing through another paper, then paused at a society page that held all the local gossip of the time. A reporter mentioned that the Kesslers had acquired a red mercury glass vase specifically for their Christmas party, but there was no photo or mention of where they'd purchased it.

Liz poked her head back in, the frown etched even more deeply on her face. "Sorry, but I have to get going. Any success?"

Maggie brought her friend up to date. "I still want to look at the last few years to see if there's any information on why Adele stopped hosting the parties."

"Don't stay up here in the cold too long, and let me know what you discover. Oh, and maybe you could check the historical society's records too. They might have something on that vase. Good luck." Liz gave Maggie a quick hug and departed.

Without Liz's cheer, it seemed even colder in the room. Maggie got up and stretched for a few minutes to get her circulation going. She found the box for the year of the last Kessler Christmas party and pulled it out, then found the right issue in December. Paper in hand, she sat at the table and read the article written by a local reporter named Beth Thomas. The story was short but was filled with vivid descriptions that included the vase. Maggie had never heard of Beth, but she hadn't lived in town long enough to know everyone. Beth certainly wasn't a reporter any longer; it was just Thad now.

Maggie rummaged through box after box but didn't come

up with any additional information about the vase or an answer to why Adele had stopped throwing her parties. Since Beth had written the article for the last party, perhaps she would have more information about the vase and why the parties had stopped.

Maggie stood and paused in the waning sunlight. The archives had become positively spooky in the dusky shadows. She wasn't about to stay there in the dark, and she had all the information the place could give her. She hurried to stow the papers, then double-checked to be sure she'd put everything back as she'd found it, even placing the chairs she and Liz had used in the same dust-free prints on the dark linoleum floor.

Back in the office, she approached Thad.

"Find everything you need?" he asked.

"Not quite. I was hoping you could give me some information about Beth Thomas."

"Beth? Now I haven't thought about her in quite some time." He tapped a finger on his chin and stared up at the ceiling.

"What can you tell me about her?"

"Late twenties when she worked part time for me. Single gal. She left shortly after my son was born. Short notice too. What with the holidays and having a new baby—I was swamped."

"Can you describe her?"

"Sure. Petite. Came up to about here." He stood and lifted his hand to his chest. "Guess that'd be about five two, five three. Darkest hair I ever saw. Her eyes were . . . I guess I never actually paid that much attention. I don't know the color."

"Did she leave a forwarding address?"

"No. I paid her last check in cash and that was it. I remember at the time thinking something was wrong, but she wouldn't talk about it. Why all the questions about Beth?"

"She wrote the article about Adele's last Christmas party. Any idea why Adele quit hosting them?"

"No, but folks speculated of course. Saying they were too costly. But you know, I always suspected that was about the time Chad started getting into trouble and she was too embarrassed to hold parties when everyone was gossiping about him."

"You don't think Beth leaving had anything to do with her covering Adele's last party, do you?"

"Can't see how it could be related, but you could ask folks around town. Someone's bound to remember that last shindig." His expression brightened. "You ever think about being a reporter?"

"Me?" She clutched her chest. "No, why?"

"You ask a lot of good questions, and if you don't mind my saying so, you're a bit nosy, which makes for a good reporter."

She was taken aback for a moment, but then she smiled. "I guess I am nosy, and I promise if I ever consider a job as a reporter, I'll come to you first."

He gave a deep, rich laugh that shook his small potbelly.

She chuckled with him. "Thank you again for your help, Thad. I made sure everything was back in its rightful place."

"You're welcome," he replied cheerfully. "Neat and nosy. A deadly combination in my book."

How ironic to mention a deadly combination when I'm working on saving a woman's life.

7

Maggie skirted the wide white columns in front of The Busy Bean. Icicles gleamed in the sun and salty ocean air rushed over the patio. She pushed through the door and was welcomed by warm air and bright colors. Daisy stood behind the coffee shop's original counter. She chatted with a trio of customers who sat on metal stools with teal vinyl seats. The mismatched chairs surrounding lemon yellow tables were nearly empty during the lull between lunch and dinner.

Daisy was invaluable when Maggie needed information about someone in town. A Southerner by birth, she had won The Busy Bean in an essay contest thirty years before, then met and married Harry. Perhaps it was her different upbringing or the fact that she was newer to the town than most, but Daisy often observed much more than those who had been in Somerset Harbor for generations. Maggie definitely needed her unique perspective now.

Maggie took a seat at the end of the counter away from the other customers to keep her conversation with Daisy private.

Daisy sauntered over to Maggie and leaned a generous hip against the countertop. "What can I get you, hon?"

"How about some tea?"

Daisy scrunched up her eyes and appraised Maggie. "You look like you could use a healthy dose of caffeine. So English Breakfast it is."

Maggie wasn't sure she needed caffeine so late in the afternoon if she wanted to sleep tonight, but Daisy had already bustled away.

When Daisy had placed the steaming cup on the counter, she pulled up a worn wooden stool from behind and dropped onto it with a long sigh. "Something tells me you need more than just caffeine. Out with it, Maggie."

With Daisy's ability to tune in to what made people tick, Maggie often thought Daisy should join Liz in counseling women at church. "I'm hoping you can give me some information about Beth Thomas. She was a reporter at the *Herald* about twenty-five years ago."

"Beth? I remember her, but only vaguely. She kept to herself, and then she took off a few years after I got here. All I know about her is that she liked her coffee black and in a to-go cup. Wait . . ." Daisy leaned forward and dropped her voice. "Does this have something to do with the key that you found?"

"How did you hear about that?"

"Please." She rolled her eyes. "James was not exactly quiet at lunch the other day. I reckon half the town knows about it by now."

When Maggie had first come to town, she'd been surprised how fast news traveled, but not anymore. She made a mental note to have a few words with Alderman Bennett about this later. "Exactly what did you hear?"

"Oh, not much. You and June went to the Kessler house. Rumor has it that the place is haunted."

"Haunted? That's news to me."

"I didn't say I believed it. I'm just telling you what I heard."

"We were there for the estate sale. Adele only passed a few weeks ago."

Daisy crossed her arms in mock annoyance. "Do you want me to tell the story or not?"

"Sorry," Maggie said, stifling laughter.

"Anyway, you and June braved your fears and entered the house to find a mob of shoppers. Everyone wanted the vase and you battled through them, pushing and shoving to get to it first. How's June's black eye, by the way?"

Maggie could only shake her head.

"Once you had the vase you took it back to your shop. It was cold and dark with a single light shining on the vase like a spotlight. You held your breath. Pulled out the greenery. A shiny key fell out." Daisy gasped dramatically and jumped to her feet in her excitement.

"Illuminated in the light it sparkled up at the two of you," she continued, her voice now low and mysterious. "You both stood in wonder, unable to move. Suddenly you touched it and an ominous feeling settled over you. You dropped the key and frantically dug through the greenery, where you found the note." She clutched her chest dramatically. "You couldn't budge. Couldn't think. When you recovered, you called the police and they raced to your shop."

She mimicked the sound of sirens and Maggie had to work even harder to keep a straight face.

"Officer Linton called out the entire force to converge on Adele's house. They found nothing, but our whole police force is on alert, waiting for anything you discover." She seemed to wilt from the storytelling performance and dropped onto the stool.

Maggie couldn't help it; she cracked up. When she could speak again, she said, "You do have a way with words, Daisy Carter."

"How do you think I won the Miss Savannah beauty contest?" Daisy patted her hair, which was pulled back with a two-inch teased bump in the rear. "The gift of gab *and* my good looks."

"Problem is, your stories are sometimes a bit bigger than the actual facts." Maggie gave Daisy the corrected version of the story, but she was pretty sure Daisy would prefer to stick with her own more colorful rendition.

Daisy leaned forward and rested her chin on her fist. "And how is Beth related to the key?"

Maggie shared details of her trip to the *Herald*. "Beth might be able to tell me more about the vase, but I have to find her first."

"I suggest talking to some of the longtime residents like Elsbeth over there. As the church secretary, she knows a lot more about what's going on in town than people think." Daisy spun on her stool. "Hey, Elsbeth. Do you remember Beth Thomas?"

Elsbeth Holdridge got up so quickly that the glasses she wore on a chain around her neck caught in the buttons on her cardigan. She fiddled with the chain as she crossed over to them. "Sure, I remember Beth. She was a reporter for the *Herald*."

"Do you know where she lives now?" Maggie tried to keep the excitement from her voice.

"She wasn't a churchgoer, so I didn't know her all that well. I did hear that she suddenly skipped town. That was . . . gee . . . let me think." She tapped her chin. "Twenty years ago?"

"Twenty-*five*," Daisy corrected. "A few years after I came to town, if I remember."

Elsbeth snorted. "And who could forget that day."

Daisy winked. "I aim to make an impression."

"Can you suggest someone who might have Beth's current address?" Maggie interrupted, sensing a lengthy banter was about to ensue.

"What about the post office? Wouldn't they have an address if she forwarded her mail?" Daisy suggested.

"Yes, but they have strict privacy policies. I don't think they'd just give out that information," Maggie said.

"You could ask around town," Elsbeth said.

Indeed she could, but few residents were out in the bitter cold. She would have to go to their homes.

If it's warmer tomorrow, I can start first thing in the morning.

With the mystery surrounding Beth's sudden departure from Somerset Harbor, she could also be involved in putting the key into the vase. It had already been a full day since Maggie had found the note; if it was a current crisis, the writer was running out of time.

Maggie glanced at the clock. If she hurried, she would have enough time to go to the historical society to search archives before their meeting at Hayward Mansion tonight. She said goodbye to her friends and tightened her collar before braving the cold again. On her way down Shoreline Drive, she greeted a few longtime residents who were hardy enough to brave the elements and asked about Beth. She received the same answer from all. They had known her, but didn't know what had become of her.

Frustration started taking hold, but it evaporated the moment Maggie laid eyes on the society's Victorian house. Bright rose paint covered most of the exterior, with white and teal trim making the place come alive. *I love this house for so many reasons.* The abundant gingerbread trim reminded her of a dollhouse she'd played with as a child, and the small round turret with a quaint parlor inside had found a special place in her heart.

Inside, Maggie climbed the curving staircase to the second floor. On the way up, she ran her hand affectionately over the dark mahogany banister. She pushed open the attic door and the cold seeped out to greet her. The worn wooden stairs reminded her of the steps leading up to Sedgwick Manor's attic and hours spent with her aunt Evelyn during her childhood, Evelyn telling her hair-raising stories about the attic. How she wished Aunt Evelyn was here with her on this search! Though they'd be hunting through dusty records, Aunt Evelyn would make the stories come to life as she'd done with the many books they'd read together when Maggie visited as a child.

Maggie pulled the string to the single light that hung from the center of the rafters. The ceiling was high enough to walk upright, and the room was filled with boxes of items used by members for promoting history in the community. She found record boxes stacked on shelves against the wall and started flipping through files dated around the time of Adele's birth. She settled in and lost herself in the many pictures and memorabilia. She'd just found something when her phone's shrill reminder alarm startled her.

She blew out a deep breath, glad no one had seen her jump. She snoozed the alarm and went back to the news article that had just caught her interest—a picture of Adele's mother posing with the vase, accompanied by a short story.

I must have missed this in the newspaper archives.

Maggie stared at the woman's dark hair and lithe figure in her luxurious-looking gown, her manicured nails resting on the empty vase. She was strikingly lovely, and her pose gave her an air of privilege. Maggie read the story, which said the family had acquired the vase from an auction house. She doubted the key had been tucked inside it back then.

Maggie's alarm yelled at her again, and she sat back. She didn't want to be late for the meeting, and she could always come back to continue her search. She reluctantly left the historical society and headed for Hayward Mansion on the east side of town.

She found her fellow historical society members already gathered in the drawing room. They stood around the tall tree, hanging colorful ornaments; storage boxes were scattered around the room. A fire blazed in the large stone fireplace, crackling merrily as it warmed the room.

"You have to tell us about the key!" Ruth demanded the moment Maggie entered the room. "And the note!"

Ina placed an ornament on a lower branch and pivoted to face them. "We've heard so many rumors." She shot an irritated glance at Daisy.

"I already told you all about it." Daisy sniffed.

Ruth scoffed. "We want the *facts*, without any added details."

"But life is so much more interesting with added details," Daisy protested.

Maggie took out the key and passed it around as she told them about its discovery and her research about it thus far.

Ina stared at the key in awe. "What do you think it's for?"

"Due to its size, I'd say a door," Fran suggested from near the fireplace, where she laid pine boughs on the wide mantel.

Ruth picked up a small silver bell. "I agree."

"But it could fit something smaller, like a trunk," Daisy offered. "Down in Georgia, there are lots of antique trunks, and I've seen big keys used to open them."

Liz carefully draped a paper streamer around the tree. "A door sounds good, but then so does a trunk. I just don't know."

"I think we need to keep our options open." June had a small box of punched-tin ornaments. "If you rule anything out this early in your investigation, you might miss something."

"Spoken like a detective." Maggie squeezed June's arm. "For those of you who think the key fits a door, why do you think it would be jeweled?"

"I know." Daisy hung a large glass Santa on the tree. "The wealthy often have things made that don't make sense to us worker bees. Adele's ancestors were well off. They could have added the jewels to a working key simply because they're pretty."

Maggie pondered Daisy's comment. "If that's the case, it might fit a special door in Adele's house."

Ina lifted her narrow chin. "I suspect if Adele's son knows about the key, he must be looking for it."

A few of the others murmured their agreement, surprising Maggie. "You don't think he's the one who has taken this woman captive, do you?"

Ina shrugged and sat down to sort through a box of battery-powered candles that they would put on the tree next. "Chad did have quite the reputation in town, so it wouldn't surprise me. It was never anything that serious when he was a teen, but maybe he got worse as he got older. Besides, as June said, we can't rule out any possibilities."

"And what about that woman?" Ruth asked. "If there really is, or was, a hostage, who do you think it could be?"

"Tell us again what the note said," Ina ordered. "Does it give a clue about who this woman might be?"

"Basically it was a cry for help from the woman who'd been kidnapped so she'd give the man the key. She doesn't know what it's for, but it involves money. She begs for help finding whatever the key opens. But there's really no indicator about who she is."

Ina shivered. "The poor woman."

"James suggested that Adele would probably have allowed her nieces to visit. What if it's one of them?" Maggie's idea kicked off a discussion about the possibilities, and the group ended up undecided on the woman's potential identity and Chad's involvement.

Fran cleared her throat as she placed a red candle among the fragrant boughs. "Are you planning to see if anyone knows Adele's nurse so you can check in with her and see if Adele had any other female visitors?"

"Good idea, Fran," Ruth said and looked at Maggie. "You could call a home nursing agency or ask at the grocery store."

"I could even talk to the pharmacist," Maggie said, catching their excitement.

"I'll be glad to stop by the pharmacy for you," Ruth offered.

"I've known Steve for forever. He'd tell me if he's met the nurse."

"I'll check in at the grocery store," Liz added.

"That would be wonderful, but do you have time for this?" Maggie asked, not wanting to tax her friends.

"Don't you worry about that," Ruth said. "But what about Chad? Word of the key is going to spread around town, and if he still has any connections here, he'll find out that you have the key and what it's worth. He'll want it back."

"Technically it's mine fair and square. I bought the vase and its contents, even though no one knew the key was in there." Maggie selected a fragile paper fan hung by gold beads, one of her favorite ornaments in the collection. "But if we end up proving it belongs to Chad, I'll give it to him."

"What I want to know is why someone added the compass to the key." June placed a glass ball on the tree and turned. "That's a little weird, right? Especially if they knew what the key was worth and that it would decrease the value."

"It could be a clue as to what the key opens," Fran offered.

"What if it's an old pirate's chest?" Ida got a twinkle in her eye. "With Somerset being a harbor town and Adele coming from a long line of shipbuilders, it seems possible to me. It could be related to shipping or even fishing."

Maggie sighed and draped the beads over the bough, the supple needles tickling her fingers. "What you're all saying is that I have quite a few directions I could take in my investigation."

"I'd keep trying to get into the Kessler house," June said as she closed empty ornament boxes for storage. "I know the place is kind of eerie, but the key could open a secret door."

Daisy rubbed her hands together. "The stories I could tell if it turned out to be for a secret door."

The women groaned in unison.

"I'm just saying." Daisy's grin widened.

"It sounds like a very good possibility," Maggie said. "And the money the woman talks about in the note could be hidden there."

"Can I see the note?" Ruth asked.

Maggie fished it from her bag and handed it over.

Ruth lifted her glasses and held the paper close. "The ink doesn't seem old."

"James suggested we test the ink, but it would take too long. Thankfully, Officer Linton has been very helpful." Maggie nibbled on her lip and wished she had more to go on.

"Doesn't matter if you figure out if it's current or not," Liz said firmly as she helped June stack boxes. "As long as there's potential for a woman to be in danger, it can't be ignored."

"You know, I've begun to think that determining the age of the paper in the vase and the identity of the woman who wrote the note isn't something I'll discover through dusty old records," Maggie said thoughtfully. "Putting my efforts into tracking down Beth Thomas, learning more about the key, and seeing inside the Kessler house would be a better use of my time."

"We can each ask around town about the key, the vase, and Beth," Fran offered. "Someone is bound to know something that can help."

Maggie retrieved the key and note and stowed them safely back in her bag. "Above all else, making sure no one is in danger comes first. I need to get into that house ASAP."

"But how?" June asked. "The curator certainly isn't going to let you in."

"I might have a way around that," Maggie said with a grin.

8

Well that was a dead end.

Maggie disconnected her call to the third nursing agency she'd phoned since she opened Carriage House Antiques that morning and went to help a customer. When she'd asked the agencies for the name of a nurse who might have been assigned to Adele, they'd all shot her down, citing privacy issues. It was all she could do to contain her frustration. It had been two days since she and June had found the note, and she felt no closer to helping its writer. She wanted to be out finding the woman, but June had asked for the day off to attend an auction for an antique store up the coast that was going out of business. Despite a mystery to solve, Maggie's commitment to the shop came first, even if June was going to spend the night and not be back until noon tomorrow. Besides, Ruth and Liz had promised to do some legwork for her today.

As she approached the front of the shop, she spotted late-morning clouds with the threat of snow hanging outside. Not that the weather had slowed her business. With Christmas in a few weeks, people needed to shop despite the weather.

A woman with lovely silvery hair stood in front of a William and Mary dresser, eyeing the silver snuffboxes displayed on its top.

"Hello! I'm Maggie. What can I help you with today?" Maggie asked.

"Harriet," the woman replied. "I'm just browsing. I've lived in Somerset Harbor all my life, and I've always loved this shop."

"We love to hear that." Maggie decided to go out on a limb. "If you've been here all your life, did you know a Beth Thomas?"

Harriet paused. "I guess. At least I knew her as well as anyone, which isn't saying much."

"What do you mean?" Maggie asked.

"She covered a fundraiser I chaired for the school, and she was very friendly. But then I'd see her in the grocery store after that, and she'd ignore me as if we'd never met." Harriet shook her head. "We're a friendly town, and it seemed peculiar to me."

"Maybe she was a private person or was afraid people would always feel like she was interviewing them." Maybe that was why she hadn't told anyone she was leaving town or where she was going. "Did you know Adele Kessler?" Maggie asked, hoping to learn more about the unidentified nurse.

"Sure." Harriet's forehead creased. "I was so sorry to hear of her passing."

"Did you know her nurse by any chance?"

"Nurse? No." Her voice grew sad. "Once Adele became a shut-in, she didn't let any of us visit."

Harriet selected an early nineteenth-century George IV sterling silver snuffbox and left. The moment the door closed, Maggie phoned James to ask for his help in getting in to see the Kessler home. His voice mail said he was out for the day, and she left a message telling him where he could find her when he got back.

Restless, Maggie set to work restocking the Christmas display at the entrance. They'd filled the area to the brim with paintings, statues, ornaments, and figurines after Thanksgiving, but items had sold quickly. She set out replacements, only partially paying attention to the display as she ran over the few facts she had about the mysteries of the key, the vase, and the note. She was interrupted several times to check out customers, which irritated her still more, though her practical side was grateful for the business. Finally, at the end of the day, she settled a lovely primitive American folk art painting in the last remaining space.

She stood back to look at the painting of skaters on a pond in front of a red mill, snow softly falling around them. She started as a mahogany Edwardian grandfather clock in the corner chimed, signaling that it was time to close the shop.

Maggie snatched her belongings, locked up, and drove to The Busy Bean. She ordered a bowl of hearty vegetable soup from Daisy, and then took a seat on a stool near the door, where she could talk to customers as they arrived and ask about Beth and Adele's nurse.

In between her interrogations, she used her laptop to search for information on women named Beth Thomas in the area. The name was common, producing a long list of search items, and she methodically worked down the list.

Finally, she hit upon two women who fit the criteria.

"Yes!" She pumped her fist into the air, and then quickly clapped the same hand over her mouth when conversations ceased and all eyes focused on her. Abashed, she waved shyly and waited until the other diners went back to their meals and their conversations. Daisy, of course, was another story. She finished pouring coffee and made a beeline for Maggie. "Out with it," she commanded.

"I've had some success." Maggie swiveled her computer toward Daisy to display the information she'd found.

Daisy studied the screen, then her head popped up, her eyes wide. "This is great. Not only one Beth Thomas but two of them right here in our county. Do you think either one is the reporter?"

"I'll have to talk to them to be sure."

I sure hope this lead pans out. Time is ticking away.

A rare frown crossed Daisy's face. "That might be dangerous, don't you think?"

"You think so? If Beth Thomas is involved, she isn't the one holding our mystery woman hostage—the note clearly refers to a man."

"But she could be partners with the man."

The hair on the back of Maggie's neck rose, but she couldn't ignore this lead. "I have to talk to these women."

Daisy was quiet, as if she was thinking how best to word what she wanted to say, which concerned Maggie, as Daisy wasn't usually the type to think before she spoke. "You're going to go see both of these women no matter what I say, but how about taking someone with you? Like James."

Maggie wasn't thrilled about the idea. What if having a man along intimidated the former reporter into silence? On the other hand, she also needed to think of her own safety. "I tell you what. I'll call them first, and if I get a bad vibe, I'll take someone with me. If I go alone, I'll leave the addresses with you so you can sound the alarm if I'm gone too long."

"It's a good compromise, I guess." Daisy's expression clearly said otherwise.

Maggie dug out her phone. "You have customers to help, and I have calls to make. Wish me luck."

Daisy gave a halfhearted thumbs-up before checking with the people at the counter.

Maggie was thankful that Daisy hadn't pressed her to take James along as her bodyguard. Daisy was usually like a dog with a bone when she wanted something.

She dialed the first Beth Thomas on the list. The phone rang five times before Beth answered with a rough "Hello?"

Maggie ignored the grumpy tone and forced herself to remain cheerful. "Is this Beth Thomas?"

She groaned. "Great, all I need is a marketing call."

"No wait," Maggie said quickly. "I'm not a telemarketer."

"Bill collector then."

"No, no. My name is Maggie Watson. I live in Somerset Harbor, and I'm trying to locate the Beth Thomas who worked as a reporter here a few decades ago."

"Wasn't me."

"You're not a reporter, then?" Maggie confirmed.

"That's what I said, lady. And I'm sick of being confused with her. Don't call me again."

There was an abrupt *click* and Maggie glanced at her phone. Disconnected.

Maggie hit redial and waited as the phone continued to ring without an answer. She left a message thanking the woman for talking to her and urging her to call if she knew anything about the reporter's current location.

Maggie sipped from her mug and worried that the second Beth might have the same issues and would hang up on her like the first one had.

I'll get nowhere if that happens.

She grabbed a notepad from her tote and jotted down the address and phone number of the second Beth. Then she trailed Daisy into the kitchen. Maggie set her mug in the dirty dish bin and spotted Daisy on the far side of the spotless kitchen talking to her cook, Jack.

Maggie joined them and took hold of Daisy's wrist. "Sorry, Jack. I've got an urgent matter to discuss with Daisy."

Maggie dragged Daisy to the doorway and handed her the note. "This is where I'm going."

Daisy glared at her. "It's nearly eight o'clock at night!"

"Then there's a pretty good chance she'll be home," Maggie said firmly.

"I still think taking someone along with you is a better idea, but make sure you check in with me so I know you're safe."

Maggie agreed, then stole back through the swinging door. She packed up her computer and supplies and ran smack into James as he walked in.

"James! I was hoping to see you."

She expected his warm, welcoming smile, but he pursed his lips and gave her a suspicious face instead. "Why do I think you want more than my company?"

"I enjoy your company," she replied, "but you're right. I need to follow up with you about a few things."

"Why don't we sit down to talk about this?" He steered her to their usual table.

"I know the police are doing all they can at the Kessler house within the limits of the law," she said before he could ask questions she didn't want to answer. "But I still don't think it's enough. I need to get into that house to see for myself that a woman isn't being held inside. Have you talked to the curator yet to see if he'll let me in?"

"Not yet. He hasn't returned my call. But I will keep trying."

"Please do your best, and please keep looking for Chad."

"Of course. Anything for you, Maggie." He sounded tired now.

"I've got to get going." She jumped up.

"Where are you off to in such a hurry?"

Maggie brought him up to speed on Beth Thomas.

He arched a brow. "Be careful, Maggie. I wish you'd let me come with you, but I won't force you."

"Thanks, James. You're a good friend."

In her car, Maggie spent the thirty-minute drive focusing on the questions she would ask Beth. By the time she turned onto a long, secluded driveway, her car's clock read that it was half past eight. Maggie eased the car down the narrow drive lined with trees that cast menacing shadows and seemed to be closing in on her. Maggie suddenly wished she'd waited until morning to come out to the boonies all alone.

Don't let your imagination get the best of you, she warned herself and concentrated on the deep snowbanks lining the road. The trees were laden with snow, making a perfect winter scene if she would just let herself relax and enjoy it.

When she reached a small clearing, her headlights revealed a saltbox-design home with the second story angling down to a single level in the back. The once-white siding was gray with age. The front door was red and chipped. She couldn't let go of her sinister feeling, so she palmed her phone in case she needed to call for help in a hurry, hoping there would be a police officer close by. She approached the worn-down house with trepidation and knocked hard enough to send little red paint chips flying.

The door opened and a petite woman appeared. Her shoulder-length hair was as black as the night outside, except for streaks of gray. A loud television blared in the background, and the smell of fried food drifted out the open door. The woman fit the general description of the reporter as described by Thad, but then the description had been so vague that many other women could fit it as well.

"Can I help you?" The woman eyed Maggie warily.

Maggie quickly explained the reason for her visit. "I'm trying to find the Beth Thomas who was a reporter at the *Herald*."

The woman took a step back, a look of concern flashing on her face before a shutter came down to hide it. "I knew her. The reporter. We're about the same age, and we often got each other's calls back in the day."

"Do you happen to know where she might be?"

"Last I knew, she was working as a reporter at the *Portland Gazette*."

"Do you know anything else about her?"

Beth raised an eyebrow. "What do you want to know?"

"Are you in touch with her?"

"No," she said shortly.

Maggie wouldn't accept her desire to stop this conversation. "Is Beth still in Portland?"

"I don't think so."

"Married with a different last name?"

She crossed her arms. "I never heard she got married. But like I said, we're not in touch."

"Is she still a reporter?"

"How should I know?"

Maggie might as well have been talking to a stone wall. This woman was not forthcoming. "What about her address in Portland back when you knew her? Did you have that in case her mail was delivered to you by mistake?"

"No, but you could check with the old mailman. He's retired now. His name's Charlie Frazier. He and my dad went to school together before he moved to Portland, and they always kept in touch."

Well, that's a little bit of help. Maggie knew she'd never get Beth's former address from the post office, but a retired worker was another thing altogether.

"Does he still live in the area?"

"As far as I know."

"Good." Maggie drew a deep breath, then pressed on. "Do you know the Kessler family?"

"Doesn't everyone in these parts?"

"Are you aware of any dealings Beth may have had with them?"

Her expression remained blank. "I know she went to their parties. We all did. Except Beth got paid to because she was working for the paper."

Okay, she's holding something back, I can tell. Maybe the two Beths have more in common than she's letting on.

Beth cleared her throat. "You never said why you wanted to talk to her."

"I didn't, did I?" Maggie replied, enjoying that she could now be the evasive one. "Is there anything else you can tell me about the other Beth Thomas?"

Beth widened her stance and clenched her jaw. "She's a good person, so whatever you think she's involved in, I doubt she's actually part of it."

"I didn't say she was involved in anything bad." Maggie watched the woman for a moment, looking for any hint of deceit. "Is there a reason you brought that up?"

Beth didn't reply, staring over Maggie's shoulder. Maggie waited and tapped her foot, but Beth kept her stoic soldier pose.

"Well, if that's all you know, I'll be on my way." Maggie handed her business card to Beth. "Thank you. And please call me if you think of anything else."

As Maggie made her way back to the car, she felt Beth watching her. She fought off her disappointment at the less-than-helpful interview by focusing on the one small lead she'd received. If Charlie could provide Beth's forwarding address, then Maggie might be able to trace Beth's movements going forward.

Maggie climbed into her car. The trees surrounding the house definitely felt menacing now. She knew she was letting her imagination go wild again, but something was off about the woman she'd just talked to, and it made her stomach tighten.

She cranked the engine and started down the mile-long driveway, keeping her eyes open for anything unusual. She wound around the curves, the shadows growing somehow deeper. By the time she made the final curve and could see the road, her heart was racing.

"Seriously, you need to calm down." She spoke out loud as she eased onto the road.

Her headlights fell on an old panel van parked in a copse of trees.

Had the ratty old vehicle been there when she'd arrived? She wasn't sure. Regardless, it was an odd place to park.

She slowed and took a good look at the vehicle. Maine's motor vehicle laws required a front license plate, but the front holder was empty. Maybe the black—or was it navy?—vehicle was a junker that stayed where it was.

She crept closer and squinted harder. She spotted a dark figure sitting in the driver's seat and jumped. Large with wide shoulders, the driver was definitely a man, but he ducked out of sight before she could decipher anything else.

That's definitely not normal. Had he followed her? Or was he there to harm Beth?

Should she get out and talk to him?

Right. Like approaching a suspicious male in a creepy van in the middle of nowhere is safe. If I survived, I think Daisy and James would fight over who got to kill me. She might be curious, but she knew better than to risk her life.

She started down the road, but suddenly a thought hit her: *What about Beth?* This guy could have been waiting for Maggie to leave so he could harm Beth. Should Maggie go back and warn Beth, or should she mind her own business?

It might be nothing, but how could she live with herself if she didn't say something?

She made a quick U-turn.

The van hadn't moved, but the man had straightened up. As she approached, he ducked down again. He was clearly up to no good. She raced back to the house. She dug a flashlight from her glove compartment and hurried up the walk. She pounded on the door, looking over her shoulder to make sure the van hadn't followed her.

Beth pulled open the door and light spilled into the darkness, easing a bit of Maggie's concern.

"Now what?" Beth demanded. "I told you everything I know."

"There's a van parked at the end of your driveway." The words flew from Maggie's mouth. "An old one. No license plate. A guy is sitting inside, and when I drove past, he hid. We should call the police."

Beth's face paled. She took a deep breath. "It's nothing to concern yourself with."

"So you know who it is?"

"As I said, it's none of your concern." She started to close the door.

Maggie shoved a foot in the way. "But we should call the police."

"You'll leave it alone if you know what's good for you."

"Do you know him?"

Beth pushed Maggie's foot out of the way and slammed the door.

"Fine," Maggie muttered as she trudged back to her car. "If she wants it like that, then I am no longer responsible. I did what I could."

She told herself that, but as she passed the van again, she couldn't help but think she'd regret not pressuring Beth further about the mysterious man.

9

Maggie paced Sedgwick Manor's library, a room she'd often found calming, but nothing was working to calm her tonight. She passed the rolling ladder she'd climbed as a child to reach books on the upper shelves. Try as she might, she couldn't let go of her conversation with Beth. Maybe she was worried for Beth. Or maybe she was wondering if she'd missed an opportunity by not marching up to the van and demanding to talk to the person who obviously wanted to hide from her.

Snickers wound between her legs and she scooped him into her arms. "What do you think, buddy? Did I miss an opportunity or did I do the right thing?"

Snickers meowed.

"You're right. It wasn't safe, and I did what I could, but still, Beth's behavior was so strange. Why wouldn't she want to call the police about the van?" Maggie sighed, her breath whispering through Snickers's fur. "Well, there's nothing I can do about that now, but I can search for articles written by Beth Thomas in the *Portland Gazette*."

She went into the adjoining office and sat at her computer. Snickers took his place on her lap. Not that she minded. He'd help keep her warm. She'd lit a fire in the library fireplace and in contrast, the office felt cool.

She found the *Gazette*'s website and plugged in Beth's name. Nothing came up in her search. Most likely, Beth had been employed with the paper before the advent of the Internet. And newspapers didn't publish all of their stories online in order to motivate people to continue buying the actual paper; perhaps

Beth had only covered the stories that didn't make it online. Maggie would have to call the paper tomorrow.

Her phone rang. She startled, and Snickers jumped to the floor, miffed at being dislodged.

"Sorry, Snickers." She glanced at the screen, which showed that Emily was calling her. Maggie's apprehension mellowed to a simmer in the pit of her stomach.

"Hey, Mom," came her daughter's chipper voice. "Sorry I'm calling so late. How are things in Somerset Harbor?"

"Incredibly busy, with Christmas coming up," Maggie replied. Busy seemed like an appropriate answer, as she didn't want to pretend everything was going well.

"What's wrong?" Emily asked.

Maggie never could fool her. She concentrated on sounding cheerful. "What makes you think something's wrong?"

"C'mon, Mom, you know you can't hide things from me. Something's up. I can hear it in your voice."

Maggie didn't want to worry Emily, but if she lied, Emily would pick up on it. "There's this mystery—"

"Not another one," Emily groaned. "How do they keep finding you?"

"Just lucky, I guess."

"Mom, I'm serious."

Maggie sighed. "I don't know how it happens, honey. I just stumble into them."

"All right, what's this one about?"

Maggie explained about the vase and her visit to Beth, but as she did so, she heard Emily's friends chatting in the background. Emily was usually full of questions, but she didn't ask many tonight. Though Maggie knew Emily was listening, she seemed distracted.

"My main objective is to find out if a woman is in danger,"

Maggie concluded. "And I think the vase and key are the best way to do that."

"Have you searched online for the key?" Emily asked.

"Yes, but I've found nothing."

"Did you take a picture of the key and upload it in your search?"

"What are you talking about?" Maggie hoped this wasn't going to be another one of those technology things that young people knew but she hadn't kept up on.

"You can do a reverse image search, where you use an actual picture to search for results."

"I'm not following you."

"Do you have your computer there, and do you have a picture of the key on your computer?"

Maggie had uploaded the picture for Nigel and Erwin. "Yes."

"Hold on a second." Though Emily must have put her hand over the phone, Maggie could hear her talking to someone about plans to go out in a few minutes. *College kids sure keep a different schedule than I do.*

"Okay, I'm back."

Emily walked Maggie through doing a search by image, instead of searching for the image with words. "That will show you if that key or a similar key has been posted anywhere."

"Oh, okay." Maggie was grateful for the knowledge but hoped she wouldn't have to use it again.

"Look, I gotta go."

"Did you call for a reason or just to check in?"

"Oh, yeah. I wanted to give you my schedule for the holidays. I'll go ahead and email it to you. Sorry to cut our call short."

"It's okay, honey. Have fun and thanks for the help."

"I love you, Mom. Bye."

"I love you too." Maggie hoped she'd kept the disappointment out of her voice as Emily hung up.

Maggie fell back against the smooth leather chair. She wished Emily hadn't been so distracted, but she was glad Emily had made friends and was taking time to be with them instead of studying nonstop. Maggie wouldn't have minded knowing more about her daughter's day-to-day life, but she felt certain that she'd raised a strong young woman who would succeed in this new world she was etching out for herself. *Richard would be so proud of her.*

Snickers hopped onto her lap, and she snuggled him close. He butted his head against her chin, and his soft fur tickled as she thought about her own new life. Somerset Harbor. Her friends. The shop, and of course, the mysteries that filled her days and kept her mind occupied. She was in many ways taking over where Aunt Evelyn had left off. Maggie felt a strong sense of purpose. That felt good after the period of aimlessness she had felt after Richard had died and before she had inherited Sedgwick Manor.

The doorbell chimed and Snickers leapt from her lap again to hide under the desk. She frowned. It was pretty late for a caller.

Could it be the man in the van?

A rush of concern kicked up her heart rate, and her senses went on high alert.

Don't be silly, she thought. If that guy meant her harm, then he wouldn't be politely ringing the doorbell.

She padded to the front door in the dark to keep her visitor from seeing her through the side window. She peeked outside, and a rush of relief erased her worry. James stood staring at the door, his arms wrapped around his body to keep warm.

She took a deep breath and blew out her lingering anxiety, then opened the door.

He pushed his hood from his head. "I hope it's not too late to stop by."

"Not at all. Come in." She stepped back and switched on the chandelier. The Swarovski crystal shone in the dark and reflected warmth into the deep corners.

He kicked the snow from his boots on the foyer mat.

"It's cold out there. How about a cup of cocoa?"

"Sounds great."

She gestured at the adjoining room. "I've got a nice fire going in the library. Head on in and I'll be there in a minute."

She made quick work of preparing the cocoa, and then loaded a tray with two Christmas mugs and a Santa plate of gingerbread men she'd baked earlier in the week.

He stood with his back to her, staring at the many volumes left by her aunt.

Maggie cleared her throat to let him know she'd returned. "Aunt Evelyn had quite a library."

He smiled when he saw her burden. "Here, let me get that."

He took the tray and set it on the small table in front of two worn leather chairs. As soon as they settled into the chairs, Snickers crossed the room and rubbed against James's black slacks, leaving small white hairs on them. James had met Snickers a few times now, but Maggie waited to see his reaction.

He chuckled and scratched Snickers behind the ears, and the cat flopped to the floor in contentment.

I always thought Snickers was a fine judge of character.

She handed James a mug. "So what brings you by?"

He took a sip and made a noise of appreciation. "I know you're eager to get into the Kessler house, so I wanted to update you on my progress with that. Well, my lack of progress. I haven't been able to locate Chad. I talked to the curator, and he's adamantly opposed to letting you inside."

She'd expected this response, but she was still disappointed. James's charm was usually so effective. It seemed not to work so well on the stubborn curator. "Did you ask the curator if he knew Chad? You know, just in case the curator wasn't being honest with me."

"Yes, but he claims not to know Chad at all. Don't worry. I haven't given up on finding him. I have a few other avenues to check out."

"I appreciate your diligence."

"He also said he didn't know Adele's nurse, but I'll keep asking around. Adele may have left something in her will for the nurse, so I'll see if can find anything out about that as well."

"Thank you," she said. "I appreciate your help."

He balanced the mug on his knee and pulled a glossy catalog from his jacket pocket. "The curator did help out by dropping this off late today. It's a catalog of Adele's items that will be sold at auction next week. The curator and his crew personally selected the best of Adele's estate to sell at auction and left the basic household items for the estate sale." He handed the catalog to Maggie.

"That explains why June and I didn't find anything of value that day." Maggie redirected her attention to the pages. The paper was thick and expensive. The curator would only go to such expense if the items inside were valuable. She started flipping through the pages to look for the key and perhaps a trunk or other item it might open. She was soon so immersed in the gorgeous antiques and their descriptions that she forgot all about James sitting next to her until he spoke.

"If you're looking for a key or the item it might open, you're wasting your time. That was the first thing I did when I got it, and there's nothing in there." He blew over the rim of his mug to cool it, sending swirls of steam rising into the air.

"I might see something you missed." She continued through the pages and ran her finger over the image of a late-1700s spinning wheel. She turned the page to see an early American oak drop-leaf table that was stained in a dark color and had a well-worn patina. Then her heart melted at a sweet pine cradle, rustic and charming at the same time.

James cleared his throat. She took it as a signal that he was getting antsy, so she forced herself to concentrate and not let her imagination take over as she flipped through the rest of the catalog. At the last page, disappointment crowded out her earlier optimism.

She closed the catalog and rested it on her knees. "You were right."

"If it's any consolation, I'd rather not be right in this case, but you should know that I usually am." A boyish grin lit his face.

She laughed then tapped the catalog. "It surprises me that there are not more items in here. Surely Adele would have had a larger collection."

"I thought the same thing, but the curator said this was the extent of the items Adele's executor had authorized for sale."

"Do you think Chad took the remaining pieces?"

"Likely, though the Chad I knew wouldn't have wanted to own 'old junk,' as he used to call it."

"But wouldn't he want any pieces that were valuable?"

"If that was the case, then he'd want to sell them and we'd see them in the catalog, right?"

"Then where is everything?"

"Sold over the years for money to live on, I suppose. Adele never worked. She lived off the family's money and investment income. In her younger days, she was a lavish spender, so she could have burned through all the money."

"I suppose so." Maggie thought for a moment. "I guess it's even more important to find Chad, then."

"Like I said, I'll keep after it." James reached for a cookie. "How did your visit with Beth go?"

She shared the details while he devoured a cookie and drank half his mug of cocoa.

He swallowed hard, and then gave her a look of disapproval. "I knew I should have gone with you. Did you call the police about the guy in the van?"

She shook her head. "I suggested it to Beth, but she just shut the door in my face. Since it was her property, it was her decision to call them if she thought she needed to. I think she knew him, but I don't have the right to pursue it since she told me to stay out of it. It could have been a boyfriend or a relative."

"I'm proud of you for letting it go."

She placed the catalog on the table and picked up her own mug of cocoa, enjoying the warmth. "Beth did tell me that the mailman at the time reporter Beth disappeared was Charlie Frazier, and she thought he still lived in town. Do you know him?"

"Charlie? Sure. He grew up around here. He moved to Portland after high school, but he visited his friends and family here all the time. Great guy. He developed some health issues a few years back and couldn't live alone any longer, so he's with his daughter in Pelican Cove."

"The small village just north of here?"

"That's the place." He reached for another cookie but stopped and cast a questioning look at her.

"Go ahead. Have as many as you want."

He patted his stomach. "I'll settle for two. Gotta watch my weight."

"I imagine you can eat most anything since you run daily."

"I wish that was the case." He took another cookie. "I know you're going to go talk to Charlie. His daughter's name is Wanda Peabody."

"You seem so certain you know me," she teased.

"I do. Or at least I think I'm getting a good idea of what

makes you tick." He watched her carefully as he swallowed a bite. "What's with the secretive smile?"

"Smile? I didn't know I was smiling."

"I'd ask what you were thinking, but I know you wouldn't tell me."

"It's nothing, really. Just that before you arrived, I was also thinking about what made me tick, and it surprised me that we were both on the same track."

He seemed to ponder her answer as he finished the rest of the cookie before standing. "It's late, and I should get going."

She saw him to the door and said goodnight before locking up tight.

Back in the office, she sipped her cocoa and returned to her laptop to finish the search Emily had taught her how to complete. Her excitement escalated as she clicked on the first link.

The page opened to reveal a silver chalice with an identical jewel pattern to the key. It appeared in an article posted in the *Portland Gazette* twenty-five years before in January. The headline read: "Valuable chalice stolen from church in Somerset Harbor."

10

The next morning, Maggie sat at the desk in the manor, sipping coffee and pondering what she'd found. Sunlight streamed in, seeming to bring clarity with it as she reread the article. There was an interview with Old Faith Chapel's pastor at that time. He said someone had smashed the window in the back of the church and stolen a chalice that had been borrowed for a special service. As of the article's publication date, the thief and the chalice both remained at large.

Maggie typed in search criteria for the chalice and learned that six months later, the police still hadn't recovered the chalice, nor had they apprehended the thief. She found no additional information after that date.

Leaning back in the chair, she pondered her discovery.

The matching jewel design with an intricate heart etched in the metal chalice suggested that the items were connected. Was the chalice somehow related to Adele Kessler too?

Maggie jotted down her questions on her notepad. Pastor David or Liz might know something about the chalice. But if Liz had seen the key, and the chalice had been brought back, surely she'd have recognized the heart and the jewel pattern. And why hadn't anyone on the historical society mentioned the chalice when she showed them the key? They had all lived in Somerset Harbor back then, and a theft of that magnitude would have been the talk of the town. Perhaps they didn't remember or even know the chalice's jewel configuration.

Questions burning in her mind, she sent a picture of the chalice to her phone so she could show it to Pastor David and Liz, then called Liz to arrange a meeting. They agreed to meet at the church in an hour, which gave Maggie just enough time to search for Wanda Peabody's phone number. With such a unique name and in such a small town, it was easy to find her phone number and address. Maggie jotted down the contact information. She would wait to call until later that morning; some people didn't like to be called early.

A thought hit Maggie. *What if Beth Thomas's hasty disappearance was related to the stolen chalice?* After all, she had disappeared the same year. Until this point, Maggie had assumed Beth had voluntarily left town, but she could have been investigating the theft, gotten too close to someone's big secret, and been murdered to make sure the story didn't get out.

Murdered.

Maggie felt a sudden chill in the air. She shivered as she gathered her coat and bag. If someone had murdered Beth Thomas, Maggie was treading in very dangerous waters, and she would need to be even more careful.

When Maggie pulled up to Old Faith Chapel, she couldn't help but smile at the welcoming little church. The building had a boxy outside and simple bell tower that showed its age in the bright morning light. The word *sturdy* always came to Maggie's mind when she saw it. She found such peace in simply looking at the building that had withstood so much since the early 1700s; it reminded her of the hardy, practical, and warm people of Maine.

She parked and paused to admire a life-size nativity scene out front. The scent of hay spread below the well-worn structure reminded her of hayrides during her childhood. Wreaths hung on the front doors with battery-operated candles mounted in the center, and she looked forward to the Christmas Eve service when they'd be lit as people strolled inside. She pulled open the wide doors, and the scent of old candle wax and furniture polish replaced the aroma of hay. Two aisles led to the front, where the original pulpit and altar stood. Tall brass candelabra held red candles at the end of each pew.

Though many churches from the same period as this one were plain and utilitarian, the pulpit and altar in Old Faith Chapel had intricate scrollwork and etchings in the shape of a cross on the front. They sat on a raised platform, and the pulpit looked out over the pews. Nearby, a tall tree stood proudly with white ornaments, and bright red poinsettias lined the stairs.

She continued down the wide plank floors through the sanctuary and out a back door to Pastor David Young's office. He and his wife both glanced up when she entered.

Liz stood and drew Maggie to a chair next to the one she'd vacated. "Your cryptic call this morning left me on pins and needles. I can't wait another minute to hear what this is all about."

Maggie settled into the stiff chair, trying to get comfortable. "Are either of you aware of a chalice that was stolen from this church about twenty-five years ago?"

The pastor, in his late fifties with a kind face and his wife's listening attitude, took off his reading glasses and closed his Bible. "We didn't live here at the time, but I know the chalice existed, and I've heard some crazy stories about it."

His confirmation of the chalice raised Maggie's curiosity. "What kind of stories?"

He held up a restraining hand. "Don't look so excited, Maggie. They're only stories as far as I can tell."

"Perhaps I could prove or disprove them."

"Perhaps," he said. "But I'm not convinced they could be proven. Rumor has it that Victor Arndt, the deacon who founded Old Faith Chapel, brought the chalice to the United States. Deacons in the early church often received a chalice during their ordination service as a sign of their new ministry, so that part of the story seems possible to me. It's the next bit where things hit the rails for me. Apparently the chalice was decorated with jewels that made it worth an unbelievable sum of money."

"That's what the newspaper article said too, but you don't believe it?"

He shook his head. "Churches have historically been poor and wouldn't possess an expensive chalice, much less give one to a deacon. Any money that would have been spent on such a chalice would have been better used in service to the Lord, and I am certain that that's what would have been done with it. I suspect if the story is true, then Deacon Arndt either brought a much simpler chalice with him, or if he did indeed possess a jeweled cup, it was likely donated by a wealthy parishioner. Or perhaps the jewels weren't real."

Maggie hadn't considered that the jewels could be fakes. "But wouldn't someone have tested the jewels to see if they were real?"

He shrugged. "There are no records of the value ever having been established."

"I always thought it was odd that they never had it appraised to insure it," Liz chimed in.

"I agree," her husband said. "I suspect that an appraisal confirming the jewels as fake would ruin the story of the chalice's heritage. Our members are proud of the church's past, and I wouldn't want to be the one who took away one of their stories."

"I understand that. Has anyone suggested possible suspects in the theft?"

"The rumor was Chad Kessler," Pastor David replied. "But the police could never prove it was him, and they never found the thief."

Liz faced Maggie. "Why all these questions about the chalice?"

Maggie dug out her phone to show them. "This is the picture from the *Herald* article about the stolen chalice."

"Yes, I've seen this before, likely in the same article," Pastor

David said. "But what does this have to do with the key?"

Maggie took out the key and laid it on the desk.

"Oh my." Liz put a hand over her mouth. "They match."

The pastor gave a low whistle. "Liz told me the jewels in the key are real. Our parishioners could be right that the chalice was valuable too."

"It would make more sense as to why it was stolen," Liz added.

"If the jewels weren't real, the thief wouldn't know," Maggie replied. "But real or fake, I need to find out how the key could be related to the chalice. Any ideas, Pastor?"

"Perhaps it's symbolic. If it was given to Arndt at the same time as the chalice, the only thing I can think of as it relates to the church is the Church of Keys doctrine, but that originated in Germany. I doubt it would be applicable to Deacon Arndt."

Maggie perched on the edge of her chair. "Would the church have any records of Arndt's arrival?"

"I imagine so. You could look through our old files," Liz suggested.

"The records are in the cellar." Pastor David stood. "I can let you in to look at them before my meeting if you like."

Maggie wasn't dressed for a day in a cellar, but there was no time like the present. She stood and smiled at Liz.

"If you don't surface by lunchtime, I'll get a nice hot lunch from The Busy Bean and you can join me up here for a cozy meal," Liz told her.

"That would be great." Maggie followed the pastor to the back of the building.

He approached a solid wood door with a heavy wood crosspiece lodged in steel brackets. He lifted the arm, and then inserted a key into a newer lock before pulling open the door. A pungent, musty odor filtered out to greet them, and Maggie was suddenly nervous.

"I wouldn't think you'd need two locks for a cellar," she joked.

"The arm is original, and you know it takes a minor miracle to change any of the original furnishings here. But at one time, the records had to be inaccessible for privacy reasons, so the compromise was to install the modern-day lock too." He flipped a light switch at the top of the stairs. A dim glow barely lit the rough-hewn stairs.

The pastor met her eyes. "Do you want me to come down with you?"

She hated to be a scaredy-cat and she knew he had a meeting, but she didn't want to be alone until she got the lay of the land. "Do you have time?"

He nodded and led her down the stairs. Maggie clutched the railing affixed to a wall of stone and mortar. When the basement opened up before her, her unease grew. The ceiling was made of rafters and rough boards. The cellar was small, maybe twenty feet square, with coarse wood shelves lining the walls. She wasn't usually claustrophobic, but now she felt cramped, which only fed her nerves.

"Not much of a basement for such a large building," she said.

"It wasn't meant for the church's use," the pastor told her. "Our meeting rooms were once the pastor's living quarters. The cellar was designed as the pastor's root cellar. These shelves held canned goods, not boxes. But as you know, space in the church is at a premium, so we have to use every inch of it."

She glanced around. Cobwebs clung everywhere. A single bulb hung from the low ceiling; weak light slithered through what appeared to be a window covered with wooden shutters. The room was even colder than the newspaper archive.

"It's not so bad," she said, trying hard to believe her own statement.

Pastor David dragged a small wooden stool from the corner

and set it in front of the far wall. He tapped a box on the shelf in front of him. "The records start here. We don't keep our current records down here or I couldn't give you access. I'm off to my meeting, which will last through lunch. You can talk to Elsbeth if you have any questions."

"Thanks." Maggie watched him go and tried to pull herself together. She had to admit the room seemed bigger without him, but it was also lonelier and creepier. Much creepier.

Get to work and the feeling will pass.

She grabbed the first box and settled on the stool. She dug through files without result other than numb fingers from the cold. She checked her phone periodically to keep track of the time. At lunchtime, she dashed back upstairs to join Liz in David's office.

"How's the search going?" Liz pulled containers from a Busy Bean bag.

"From what I've seen so far, the records don't go back to the earliest days, but start in the 1890s. I found notes that said the earlier records were lost in a flood. The chalice has been mentioned as related to Deacon Arndt, but I've yet to see anything that proves he brought it with him. There's no mention of the key at all."

"You poor thing." Liz squeezed Maggie's knee. "You've spent so much time looking at papers the last few days."

"And I'll be looking at more. I figure the historical society will have additional information, and there could even be more records at the newspaper."

"I'll be glad to help with either or both of those, if you want." Liz opened lunch containers that held warm roast beef sandwiches, then dug in a paper bag for to-go cups of vegetable soup. "Salted caramel sounded good to me today," she added, handing Maggie a cup of the specialty blend.

Maggie gulped the coffee. "How are your ornaments coming for the Hayward Mansion?"

Liz swallowed a bite of her sandwich. "I've set my goal to complete three every day, and I'm right on schedule."

"I wish I could say the same thing, but I know June and I will get them finished." She dipped into her soup, which warmed the bits of her the coffee had missed.

"Oh, I drove by the mansion today and saw Harry Carter putting up the outside Christmas decorations. Ruth chose twinkling white lights, and he was stringing them around the eaves. There was also a large star on the gable." She swirled her coffee. "He still has the trees and walkway to do, but I bet he'll finish this afternoon."

Maggie took a sip of her soup. "I'm sure Ruth will have it all lit up for the meeting tonight."

Liz peered at Maggie. "How do you find time to do everything and then investigate these mysteries too?"

"Sometimes I get so caught up in my investigating that I let other things go," Maggie confessed. "I don't know how you keep up with all the church events."

"This time of year can be a challenge, but I wouldn't trade it for anything." A warm smile tipped her lips. "Hey, before I forget. I was thinking on my way to get lunch. Why don't you call the *Portland Gazette* and ask about Beth Thomas?"

"Thanks for reminding me. I had planned to, but I forgot about it after finding out about the chalice," Maggie said as she polished off her sandwich.

Liz peeked at her watch as she tossed her trash into the garbage can. "I have to run. I hate to leave you here, but I have an appointment."

"Is it okay if I stay here to make that call to the *Gazette*?" Maggie asked.

"Oh sure. David has meetings all day, so you should have plenty of privacy." Liz waved a hand. "See you tonight."

When she was alone, Maggie pulled out her phone and

dialed the *Portland Gazette*. "I was hoping to speak to someone about one of your reporters."

"Hold please," the harried woman said.

An old Beatles tune played in her ear as she waited, and Maggie tried to hum along, but her heart wasn't in it. When a man answered, she rushed right into her story.

"I'm sorry," he said, "but I can't give out any personal information about our staff."

She'd expected this response, but she wouldn't let it deter her. "Can't you at least tell me if Beth used to be a reporter for the *Gazette*?"

"Sorry. As I said, no personal information."

"But that's public information. I could come to Portland and look at your archives to see if she worked there."

A drawn-out sigh filtered through the phone. "Fine. She was a reporter her, but that's all you're getting out of me. Now if you'll excuse me, I have work to do."

He hung up abruptly, but Maggie didn't mind. She now knew that Beth Thomas had once worked at the paper in Portland, which meant she had plausibly lived there as well.

Her hope renewed, she dialed Wanda Peabody, who answered on the third ring. Maggie explained her reason for wanting to talk to Charlie.

"I'm sorry." Wanda sounded like she honestly meant it, unlike the man from the *Gazette*. "I know my dad would be happy to help you, but he has Alzheimer's, so I can't promise he'll be able to remember."

Maggie's revitalized hope wavered a bit, but she continued. "Would you mind if I stopped by tomorrow to talk to him just in case?"

"No problem. Afternoons are usually better for him if you can make it then."

"How about two o'clock?"

"Perfect."

Maggie took a moment to think about Charlie and how she might help jar his memory if he was having an off day. "I'll bet he used to eat Daisy's famous muffins from The Busy Bean when he was in town."

"He did. His favorite was banana nut."

"I'll bring a few along unless he has dietary restrictions."

"He'll love them. See you tomorrow."

After Wanda hung up, Maggie definitely felt like humming, and the Beatles tune from her call to the *Gazette* came out in a joyful sound—at least in her own ears. She decided she could stand a few more hours going through records in the cellar, especially since it was now the fourth day since she had found the note, and the chalice was the best lead she had to help the writer. Even the cave-like feeling of the basement didn't daunt her, and she kept humming as she dug through box after box.

Hours later, a much quieter, colder, and more tired Maggie pulled out the last box. The sun had fallen and any warmth from it had long ago disappeared. At some point during the afternoon, she had stopped humming, though she wasn't sure when.

She closed the last box and stretched. She'd located little information about the chalice, but she needed to grab some dinner, feed Snickers, and get over to the Hayward Mansion to meet with the historical society.

She put her journal filled with her notes of dates and events she'd recorded back into her bag and stood. Her legs were stiff from the cold, and she walked woodenly toward the stairs. It didn't take her long to notice that someone had closed the door at the top of the stairs.

Whoever closed it must have done so silently, as she hadn't heard a thing. Surely it was a mistake. Someone had probably seen it propped open and closed it out of habit.

Then the eeriness of the cellar at night—ten times what it was during the day—took hold. What if someone had intentionally shut her in?

Panic grew in her, and she scrambled up the stairs, struggling to make her cold muscles cooperate. It took far too long to make the journey to the upper landing.

"Please don't let it be locked," she prayed.

She shoved at the rough-sawn wood.

The solid door didn't budge. Not a fraction of an inch.

She was trapped in the cellar.

11

Maggie set down her bag and pushed harder, pressing against the unyielding wood with every ounce of strength she could muster.

Nothing.

"No!" she cried out and kicked the door in frustration. "Please, no." She slammed her fists into the wood over and over again until her hands ached.

"Hello?" she shouted. "Is anyone out there?" She pressed her ear to the door.

No one. Not a peep.

She fumbled in her bag for her phone. The screen showed no signal.

"It has to work, it just *has* to!" She held it out. "Please, please, please, just one bar."

But she had none.

Panic sank its claws deeper.

She hurried back down the stairs and raced around the basement with her phone outstretched, watching for a change in the bars. The first bar filled in. She came to a stop and stared at the screen. It disappeared again.

Maybe if she climbed up by the window. She tested the sturdiness of the shelf and decided to try it.

She pulled herself up to the first shelf where she stuck her foot between the boxes. She heaved her body to the upper shelf and reached as far as she could with her phone. Still no signal.

Fine. Perhaps she could open the window and get out that way. She pocketed her phone and yanked on the shutter, but it didn't budge. She changed her angle and tried again. No luck. *It must either be locked or stuck.*

She heard a noise outside and peered through the slats. An old van sat out front. Not just any old van, but the one she'd seen last night at the end of Beth's driveway. There was still no license plate, just rusty bolts where it should be. The lights were out and the windows fogged.

Was the same man inside? She'd thought he'd been at Beth's house for Beth, but what if he was watching her? Had he locked her in the cellar?

She dug out her phone and opened the flashlight app, then ran the beam over the shutters on the window. They were sealed shut with a nail every few inches.

No. Please, no.

She needed to find another way out. She dropped back to the floor and used her flashlight to make a more detailed search of the area. Something scurried away from her light where the shelves joined. She refused to think about what it could be. Her flashlight's beam landed on a short length of galvanized pipe under the shelves.

"Yes!" The metal would be perfect to bang against the door or on the shutters until someone heard it.

She pulled all the boxes from the shelf to reach the pipe wedged in the back. She closed her eyes and pushed her hand through cobwebs, hoping they were old and no spiders lived there. She wrapped her fingers around the cold metal, braced her feet on the shelf, and pulled with all of her might. At first, it didn't budge, and tears threatened. But suddenly it came free and she tumbled back to the ground. She lay stunned for a moment until visions of the creature that had scurried away came rushing back, forcing her to her feet before the actual animal crawled out of the shadows and skittered over her.

"Please let someone hear me," she prayed as she mounted the stairs.

She tried the door again, hoping she'd made a mistake earlier, but it still didn't shift. She pounded with the pipe and shouted until she was hoarse, but to no avail.

Who would do this to me?

Word had spread around town that she was looking into the mysterious key. Could the person who had kidnapped the note writer also have locked her in so he could come back later when everyone was gone and take the key from her? Was it the guy in the van?

She slammed the pipe against the door a few more times, and then checked her watch. Nearly seven and time for the historical society meeting. Surely they would miss her and Liz would think to look in the cellar. Yes, that could happen, but Maggie couldn't count on it and do nothing in the meantime.

A light flashed through the shutters. She charged down the stairs and climbed up to look. The van had backed out and was driving away. She saw other headlights in the distance.

Someone was coming. She raised the pipe overhead and slammed it against the wood.

"Help!" she screamed, forcing her voice to cooperate one last time. "I'm locked in the cellar!"

In the distance, she heard the cellar door opening.

"If you think you can vandalize the church without consequences, you're mistaken," Pastor David's voice boomed from above. "I've called the police."

She tried to call to him, but her raw throat expelled his name in a whisper. She forced her cold feet toward the stairs.

The door started to close.

"Pastor David," she rasped again.

The door paused.

"It's Maggie." She had no idea if he heard her, but she started up the stairs toward the warmth and the light.

The opening widened, and she was soon at his feet.

"Maggie?" he asked in astonishment.

"Locked in," she whispered.

"Oh, my goodness, Maggie, it *is* you." He hurried down the top few stairs to her side. "What happened?"

"Someone locked the door."

"Let's get you out of here." He gripped her under the elbow and helped her out of the basement and into his office. "Thank the good Lord that I had to come back for a meeting tonight. Between you and me, many of them can be a waste of time, but I've never been more thankful to be here."

She nodded but was too exhausted and shaken to speak.

Sirens sounded in the distance.

"That will be the police," the pastor said. "I'll meet them, and then get you a nice cup of tea."

Maggie tried to get comfortable in the stiff wooden chair and waited for the warm air to seep into her bones. She must have fallen asleep; the next thing she knew, Officer Linton was standing over her.

"Ms. Watson," Officer Linton said. "Are you up to telling me what happened?"

"I'm sure it's nothing but a misunderstanding," Pastor David interjected as he handed her a mug.

She took a sip and savored the warm liquid rolling over her parched and irritated throat.

"Our janitor likely locked the door as he closed up the building." Pastor David offered her an apologetic look. "I'm sorry, Maggie. I got so caught up in my day that I never told him you were working in the cellar."

"You really think this is as simple as him locking up for the night?" Officer Linton asked.

"Absolutely. Since those kids broke in a few months ago and vandalized the church, he's been fastidious about making sure every door is locked. They came in through the cellar window and that's why we nailed the shutters closed."

"If it was the janitor, wouldn't he have turned out the cellar light?" Maggie pointed out, her voice barely above a whisper.

"He would have." A hint of concern lingered in the pastor's tone.

"Didn't you notice the door was locked before you left?" Officer Linton asked.

"Yes, of course, but I assumed Maggie had gone home." His shoulders fell. "I'm so sorry, Maggie."

"Not your fault," Maggie whispered and took another long drink of the tea. "I'm thinking it's related to the key and the vase. Most everyone in town has to know by now that I'm investigating the key. Stands to reason that someone capable of abducting a woman would know too. I saw a van outside." She described the van and explained how she'd seen it at Beth Thomas's house as well.

Officer Linton frowned at her. "If this man is really tailing you, and I'm not saying he is, then you need to be more careful. That key is valuable, and I don't doubt that this person will take extreme measures to get it."

12

With June scheduled to come in at noon, Maggie worked alone in the shop all morning, but very few customers needed assistance. Maggie used the time to make ornaments for the Candlelight Home Tour until she could make no more. She got up and puttered around the Carriage House, moving a green-and-red leaded glass shade to the Christmas display, staring at it, and relocating it again. Dissatisfied, she set it back in its original location, then grew frustrated and left it there. She simply couldn't focus on anything. She was exhausted from trying to fight her way out of the cellar the night before and then reliving the experience all night long.

She peered out the window where the day had dawned sunny and clear. The weather report had promised above-freezing temperatures today, as Somerset Harbor was used to. Protected from the coastline, they didn't often see as much snow or extreme cold as inland states, but this winter had started with weather that would challenge even the Abominable Snowman.

She spotted June hurrying toward the shop, and Maggie opened the door to welcome her.

"I'm so glad the weather has lightened up." June held out her jacket. "I barely even need this old thing."

Maggie smiled a welcome. "Don't tell Daisy that. She may have lived here for years, but even after all this time, she can never get warm, and she fears she'll catch a cold." Her voice was still scratchy this morning, but at least she could speak above a whisper.

"She's pretty vocal about winter. Oh, I ran into Ruth on the street. She was on her way to the historical society to do some paperwork. She offered to help you go through the records if you'd like."

"I might take her up on it so I'm not alone in a space where I can be locked in."

"Ruth told me about that. It must have been terrifying." June squeezed Maggie's hand and stowed her items under the counter. "Didn't the ladies miss you at the meeting? Especially Liz? I would have if I'd been there, but Kurt had a bug, so I was home with him."

"Liz missed the meeting to visit a friend in the hospital, but the others noticed. But by that time, Pastor David had returned for his meeting." Maggie sighed. "When I saw the van, I was so scared."

"I'm not good with small spaces to begin with. If it had happened to me, I'd have really freaked out."

"I think it's best if I try to forget about it."

"Of course. Anything I need to know before you go?"

Maggie shook her head and grabbed her jacket. "Give me a call if anything comes up. Otherwise, I'll see you at the meeting tonight."

Maggie paused on the sidewalk to enjoy the warmth of the sun. People flocked to the streets, the atmosphere almost celebratory after the harsh cold of the last several days. She'd have loved to take a long walk along the harbor and bask in the sunlight, but she had to go see Charlie Frazier today. She'd settle for a quick walk to The Busy Bean to pick up a box of Daisy's famous banana nut muffins. For once, the place was nearly empty and Daisy was out running errands, so it took Maggie only a few minutes to purchase the muffins.

As she went outside, she spotted James pulling into the parking lot. She'd have time for a quick chat but nothing more.

A crease appeared between his brows when he saw her. "I'm glad to see your incident last night hasn't left any physical effects."

So he's heard.

"How did you find out about it?"

"Ah, Maggie. This is Somerset Harbor, remember? I'm sure Elsbeth had the phone lines buzzing by eight this morning, and then all it took was for Daisy to hear the news."

"She told you when you stopped for your morning coffee after your run."

He arched a brow. "I'm far too predictable. I think I need to change things up to keep you guessing."

She chuckled. "I appreciate you stopping by to check on me, but other than sore muscles I'm fine."

He stood back and watched her carefully. "Please tell me you've taken the incident to heart and are going to be far more careful going forward."

"I'm surprised you're not going to encourage me to leave the investigation alone."

"Would it do me any good if I did?" he asked drily.

"No."

He sighed. "What are your plans for this afternoon?"

"First I'm going to visit Charlie, and then I'll search records at the historical society with Ruth. Nothing dangerous."

"Tell Charlie I said hello."

"I will, but Wanda said he's suffering from Alzheimer's so I'm not sure he'll remember you."

"Alzheimer's? I'm sorry to hear that." James ran a hand over his hair, leaving little tufts standing at attention. They shared a moment of silence before he said, "I should get going. I have a consult on restoring a home down the coast. A perfect example of an untouched, early seventeenth-century Cape Cod cottage. You don't see those much anymore. I wish you could come with me. You'd love it."

"You could show it to me once you finish the restoration."

"Sure, I'd be happy to, if they hire me for the job." He jingled his keys. "Which, if I'm late, they probably won't."

She bid him goodbye and strolled back to Sedgwick Manor to pick up her car. For the first time in days, Maggie's mind cleared as the pulsing ocean and sharp craggy rocks on her drive to Pelican Cove captivated her attention. When she reached the small village, her GPS directed her into town and away from the beautiful scenery, and her focus came back, along with her sense of purpose; she had found the note five days ago. Time must be running thin for her poor note writer.

Wanda's house sat on the main street between an old-fashioned barbershop and a small café. To her surprise, Maggie found herself in a lovely yarn shop instead of a residence. She immediately fell in love with the place. She didn't knit, but Wanda had decorated with an eclectic selection of early American antiques, a sure way to Maggie's heart. Maggie wandered around the room, stopping at a corner wall with rusty and worn tools that included a pitchfork, several different-sized hand drills, and a garden trowel. Perhaps Charlie's father or grandfather had used these tools. She couldn't imagine being in Wanda's position or what it must be like to see a father go through such difficulties. She made a mental note to call her own father, as she hadn't talked to him in too long.

A large woman appeared behind the counter from a back room. "Hello! I thought I heard someone out here. I'm Wanda. Are you Maggie?"

"Yes. I'm sorry. I thought you lived here."

"Oh, we live above my shop." She opened a door behind the counter. "Dad's in the back. He spends most of his day down here with me. Before we go in, though, I should warn you. It's been a bad day."

Maggie held up the pastry box. "I hope the muffins will help."

"It's possible. The senses of taste and smell have been known to stimulate memories with Alzheimer's patients, but I've never seen it work with Dad."

"You have a lovely store, by the way. I love the ambience," Maggie said as she followed Wanda through the door.

"Thank you." Wanda beamed. "Most of the items on the walls and the shelving are from my dad. He was a collector, and we cleaned out his many sheds together. On good days, the items bring him comfort." Wanda led Maggie into a room that held comfortable chairs arranged in a circle. "I reserve this space for people who want to sit and knit. Makes the days less lonely for me *and* Dad."

A man with stooped shoulders and a full head of silvery hair sat in one of the ladder-back chairs at a round oak table. Stacks of envelopes lay next to him. He cast a vacant stare at Maggie, and then regarded Wanda with no hint of recognition.

"Locals bring their junk mail in, and on bad days, he'll sort the envelopes for hours on end. It seems to comfort him." She squatted next to him. "I have a visitor for you, Dad."

He squinted up at her. "Valerie?"

"No, it's Wanda."

His face scrunched up in confusion.

Wanda met Maggie's gaze, pain in her eyes. "Sometimes his mind travels back to the past and he thinks I'm Mom."

He peered at Maggie through thick glasses. "Don't know her."

"You're right, Mr. Frazier, you don't know me."

Wanda beckoned Maggie to come closer.

She did so and held out the muffins. "I brought your favorite banana nut muffins from The Busy Bean."

"Don't know The Busy Bean," he grumbled.

Wanda took the box and opened it in front of him. A small smile started on his face, then fell away. Wanda took out a large muffin and held it closer. "Take a whiff, Dad. You love these, remember?"

He sniffed and reached for the muffin. He took a big bite and the smile reappeared.

"Good."

Wanda sat in the chair next to Charlie. "Dad, do you remember The Busy Bean coffee shop where Maggie got the muffins? It's in Somerset Harbor, where you used to live."

He peered up at Wanda. "Valerie?"

"No, I'm Wanda." Maggie heard an unuttered sigh in Wanda's voice.

"Uh-huh." He swallowed, then took another bite.

Wanda bent closer to him. "How about a woman named Beth Thomas? She was on your mail route. Do you remember her?"

He continued to chew and tapped a stack of mail on the table. He swallowed again, and Maggie held her breath, waiting for his answer.

"Mail." He went back to eating his muffin.

Wanda tried asking the same question in many forms but finally shook her head and stood. "I'm sorry. He's not up to it today. I'll ask him again in one of his lucid moments and call you if he remembers Beth. Even if he can't help you, you've made his day better, and I thank you for that." Tears formed in Wanda's eyes, and Maggie felt her own eyes filling.

"Thank you for your time," Maggie said. "I hope he enjoys the rest of the muffins."

Wanda escorted her to the door. "At least you had a nice day for the drive."

"I did indeed." Maggie thanked Wanda again and got back into her car.

Despite yet another roadblock in the investigation, Maggie chose not to let disappointment cloud her drive home. Instead, once she merged onto the coastal highway, she took the time to pray for Charlie and Wanda. Wanda's love for her father was obvious, and she had a long road ahead of her.

Out of nowhere, a van roared up behind Maggie, shocking her back to the present. She glanced in the rearview mirror. For a split second, she thought it was the van from Beth Thomas's house.

"Don't be so dramatic," she told herself firmly. She blinked a few times, and then looked again.

The van was old, navy blue, and had no front plate, just like the panel van at Beth's house—and the one she saw through the cellar window.

Had the mysterious man followed her here?

She'd been too busy looking at the scenery on the drive up to notice. She checked again. Yes, it was the same vehicle.

Fear shot through her body.

Don't panic. She tried to force her mind to stay calm and searched for an escape route in the event that he tried to ram her car.

Her eyes lingered on the steep drop-off on the ocean side. One slam of his vehicle into her rear bumper and he could push her off the cliff to certain death without much of a struggle. At least she was heading south now, so she was traveling in the interior lane. Still, perspiration coated her palms and her mind was a jumbled mess. If she hadn't had such a desperate grip on the wheel, her hands would have been shaking.

Think, Maggie, think.

First she had to get off the highway as soon as possible. She looked ahead for a turnoff and spotted a sign for a county road about a mile ahead, which she could reach in a little over a minute. She could do that.

Her eyes were drawn to the rearview mirror as if being pulled by a magnet. Was she imagining things or was the van getting closer?

She squinted at her mirror. He was definitely closer. Her panic escalated.

She couldn't make out the driver clearly, but she could see it was a man and he was alone.

Her wheels drifted off the road. The gravel grabbed them, pulling her toward the ditch. She yanked the wheel, righting her car. She searched out the windshield until she could see the turnoff ahead. She had to take the van by surprise or he'd.simply exit with her.

Nearing her turnoff, she chose not to signal, then stomped on her brakes, cranked the wheel, and flew across the painted white lines at the last second. She worried for a second that she would roll her car, but she made the corner and zoomed down the road. Her GPS device announced that it was recalculating.

"Make a U-turn three hundred feet ahead," the voice commanded.

"Right, like I'm going back to the highway." She picked up even more speed and started to relax . . . until she heard an engine in the distance.

Her gaze shot to the mirror. The van raced toward her, rapidly closing the distance between them. He was indeed following her.

Panic reared its ugly head again, and she couldn't fight it.

Now what?

13

The van continued to roar toward Maggie. She held her breath, expecting the man to ram her bumper any second. He eased off the gas about two car lengths behind her car and hung back.

Maggie let out her breath. He might not be trying to run her off the road, but she no longer questioned whether he was following her.

She took a look around. No obvious way out. She whipped around corners in hopes the van wouldn't follow, but he continued to tail her. The GPS voice kept telling her to return to the main road, but she had no desire to risk the drop-off again.

She continued on, driving away from the coastal highway. The van followed at a distance, and they traveled that way for some time. She managed to hold her panic at bay and nearly rejoiced when she saw a scenic overlook ahead. A plan formulated in her mind.

"Stay calm," she ordered herself. She would have to time it perfectly.

She approached the overlook. Mentally apologizing to her car and promising it a tune-up soon, she hit the brakes, yanked the wheel, and slid to a stop on the turnout. The van couldn't react quickly enough and shot past. She confirmed that the paneling on the sides matched the van at Beth's house. She also checked for a rear plate, but there wasn't one.

Maggie didn't sit and wait for him to whip around and get behind her again. She checked for traffic and floored the gas pedal. Her little Jetta zipped onto the road after the van. She tailed him all the way to the city limits where he continued down the road, and she exited onto Shoreline Drive. Pedestrians enjoying the day still filled the streets, and she had to slow way below the speed limit.

"Move, move, move," she growled at the people in the crosswalk, though they couldn't hear her.

She parked outside the police department and ran for the door. She charged across the foyer to Paula Ellis, the receptionist.

"Paula, help," Maggie panted. "A man in a van was following me. I need to speak to an officer."

"Calm down and I'll get the officer on duty." Paula sounded as if it was highly inconvenient for Maggie to be there with a crisis.

Perhaps this situation wouldn't terrify Paula, but Maggie was unnerved. She paced the room until the door opened and Officer Linton came to meet her.

"How can I help you, Ms. Watson?"

"A man in a van was following me. The same van from Beth's house and the church last night."

"No plates again?" he asked.

"No. Not on the front or back. But it's an old van like you see in those old beach movies—navy blue with the fake wood paneling on the sides. There can't be too many of those around here, especially without plates. Even if there is more than one, the odds of seeing three of them in as many days are ridiculous."

"You have a point." He appraised her. "Can you tell me how you know he was following you?

"I made sudden turns and took a roundabout route through the countryside, and he followed me the whole time. I finally pulled onto a scenic lookout. He was following too close so he had to pass me by. Then I followed him all the way to town. He kept going." She grabbed Officer Linton's arm. "If you hurry, you could get a county deputy to intercept him farther south."

Officer Linton slowly extricated his arm. "I'll give them a call and tell them to be on the lookout for the van. If it doesn't have license plates, they can make a stop and obtain the driver's information." His tone was reassuring. "I'll also mention it to our team, and we'll keep an eye out for the van and stop him."

"You'll share his name with me if you do stop him, right?"

His jaw tightened. "We have privacy issues to contend with, but if Chief thinks the name can be shared, he'll do so."

"Thank you."

"I'll also send a patrol past your house on a regular basis to make sure everything is okay." He smiled, but it seemed forced. "Now if you're okay, I best get those alerts out."

"Yes, I'm fine," she replied, her adrenaline ebbing. "I appreciate your support."

He pivoted and marched back through the door.

Left alone with Paula, Maggie couldn't decide what to do next. She'd planned to look through the historical society archives yet today, but she was still shaken and needed to calm down before she could concentrate on an exhaustive task.

A Christmas carol came through the overhead speaker, reminding her of the approaching holiday. What with making ornaments and the mystery to solve, she'd had no time to decorate the manor. Emily loved Christmas, and Maggie didn't want her daughter to come home to a barren house. Besides, Maggie loved decorating, especially with Aunt Evelyn's antique ornaments. She could put up a few items while she was trying to calm down and accomplish two goals at one time.

She rushed out the door and barreled straight into James. The collision sent her reeling, and she nearly fell.

He caught hold of her arms. "What's wrong? What's happened?"

"It's nothing."

"Maggie, you just came out of the police department. And

nothing doesn't put that look in your eyes. You're a strong woman and it takes a lot to scare you."

"Really, it's nothing. I was just followed by that same man in his van. That's all."

He crossed his arms. "I'm not going anywhere until you tell me the whole story."

"Please," she said. "Once I get home I'll be okay."

"Fine." He held out his hand. "I'll drive you. Keys, please."

"I really don't—"

"The longer we argue, the longer it will take for you to get home." He wiggled his fingers.

She gave in and handed over the keys, and then climbed into the passenger seat.

He adjusted the driver's seat for his longer legs, and she was pleased when he didn't try to elicit details about her harrowing drive. At the manor, she allowed him to see her to the door. She unlocked the deadbolt and was about to say goodbye when he pushed past her and into the foyer.

"Go sit down and I'll make you a cup of tea." He didn't wait for her agreement but took off for the kitchen.

Chagrined, she stared after him. She couldn't make him leave other than forcibly throwing him out the door, but that would never happen; he was stronger than she was, even when her bones hadn't become jelly. Plus, she was too mentally exhausted to argue.

The afternoon sun would still be shining through the office window, so she went into the office and collapsed on one of the old leather chairs. She stared out the window and wondered if she had overreacted.

The experience came flooding back—the van trailing behind her, the roar of the engine as he came closer, death waiting at the bottom of the drop-off.

Her heart picked up speed, and her hands started trembling again.

"A good cup of tea will help," James said from the doorway.

She shot up in her chair.

"Hey," he said soothingly. "It's just me."

"I know, I . . ."

He set the mug on the table and took a seat across from her. "Now tell me what happened to upset you so much."

She told him about the van, sticking to the facts and trying to keep her emotions in check.

"Have you had a chance to think about this man's identity and why he's following you?"

"No, especially since the second Beth Thomas I've talked to isn't even related to my investigation."

"As far as you know."

"Are you saying you think she might be the reporter?"

"Perhaps." He fell silent, letting her mull it over.

She was thankful for the quiet as she considered the possibility that this Beth could indeed be the woman she'd been looking for. "She did fit the physical description Thad gave me of the reporter," Maggie said slowly. "She seemed startled by my questions at first, but she didn't appear to be lying to me."

"Some people are good liars. Especially if they have something important to hide."

"Maybe I should talk to her again."

"If she *is* lying, you're not going to get her to tell the truth without a compelling reason."

"True." Maggie sighed in frustration.

"Besides, that's where you first encountered the van, right? The creep could be at her house again by now, and I'd rather you wouldn't go back there."

"I'd rather not go back there, either, and I won't unless I find that compelling reason you mentioned."

"Good." He clapped his hands together and leaned forward. "What will you do now?"

She drew in a deep, cleansing breath and let it out. "Take a break from the mystery for a few hours and decorate the Christmas tree that was delivered last week."

"Would you like some help?"

"You?"

"You sound shocked." He smiled. "I can go if you don't want my help."

"No, it's just . . . I know you're busy and . . ." She shrugged.

"I'm not too busy for this." He took her hand and tugged her to her feet then handed her the cup of tea. "Drink this, will you? I worked really hard on it."

Maggie was caught off guard by the hint of laughter that made its way past the lump in her throat, but she recovered enough to escort him back to the foyer.

The two-story room was open to the landing on the second floor. A perfectly shaped balsam fir stood fifteen feet tall in the middle of it.

James stopped and stared up at the tree. "She's a beauty. I don't know how I didn't notice it when I came in."

Maggie sipped her tea and took a long look at the tree too. The dark green long-lasting needles, slender form, and pleasing fragrance that it would give off for weeks made a balsam fir a perfect Christmas tree. And as a bonus, they were locally grown; Nate Gregory owned the Christmas tree farm and had handpicked this one for her home.

"I'm guessing these are filled with decorations." James had reached a stack of bins on the far side of the room.

"Yep. And there's another half dozen of them in storage."

He groaned. "What have I gotten myself into?"

"Too late to back out now."

He opened the first bin and pulled out a box of antique glass ornaments. "My mother always had a strict order we had to follow when we decorated the tree. Granted, you have to put the lights up first, but are you one of those people who has a certain place for each ornament or can we put them up freestyle?"

"Freestyle works for me." She set down her mug. "But I always save the tree topper for last. This year I'm also saving the angel you gave me so I can find the perfect spot for her." She thought about the fragile glass angel that he'd given her last month. He'd said the ornament was a belated housewarming gift, but she suspected it was as an apology for a disagreement they'd had.

"I considered putting her on top of the tree, but I have a treasured old star I can't abandon."

"Okay. Let's get to it." James withdrew a long string of lights from a bin.

Maggie went to the old Victrola phonograph in its mahogany cabinet in the corner and put on a Christmas record. The music crackled over the speaker, but Maggie wouldn't listen to Christmas songs any other way in this room; it brought her aunt Evelyn into the room with her.

She opened a bin where bright red glass Santas competed for space with blue icicles, striped and glittery balls in every color imaginable, and Dresden star ornaments in rich gold and white. She joined James as he picked up a pair of wooden Santas. They worked in comfortable silence. Occasionally, one would share a Christmas memory, and soon it was time to put up the star and place the angel.

Maggie had brought out a tall ladder for their upper ornaments, and James headed for it. Clearly, he thought it his job to put up her tree topper. She wasn't about to ruin the peaceful interlude in her otherwise crazy life with a silly quarrel.

She drew out the star and admired it. Though it had lost some gold glitter over the years, it still sparkled in the glow of nearby lights. She handed it to James, and he climbed the ladder, seeming as comfortable as a firefighter.

Once it was set in place and had been adjusted to her satisfaction, he shimmied down and they stood together for a moment before she removed the fragile glass angel from the box. The clear glass angel had gossamer wings that could snap off if not handled delicately. In fact, James had already repaired the ornament once before.

She approached the tree and found the perfect spot at eye level. She glided the angel's hanger onto the branch and stood back to admire it.

"Perfect," James said from right behind her.

She faced him. "Thanks for your help. I love decorating trees, but sharing the decorating of my first tree in Somerset Harbor will make it more memorable."

"You know me—I aim to please." He grinned.

"Said like an alderman who's stumping for reelection."

She expected him to dispute her comment, but he didn't respond. After a moment of intense silence, she grew uncomfortable standing so close to him. Thankfully the record ended and she had an excuse to move away to switch it off.

Suddenly he blurted, "Dinner. What about dinner?"

"I plan to eat it," she joked as her stomach leapt to her throat. They had eaten together before, but this time there was something different in the arrangement.

"We could go out and grab a bite together." He sounded uncharacteristically tentative.

She checked her watch. "I have a historical society meeting

soon, so I'm just going to make a quick omelet or something here."

"I like omelets . . ."

"Would you like to stay for dinner, James?" she asked, trying not to laugh.

"I thought you'd never ask." He took off for the kitchen. She stared after him, amused.

As they cooked and ate, he insisted they talk about anything other than the mystery. Normally she would have dwelled on it as it weighed heavily on her mind, but she realized that the time away from the intensity of the search for this mystery woman would make her more productive once she resumed the hunt. She tried to ignore the small voice in her head that scolded her for taking a break when someone's life could be in danger.

When it was time for her meeting, James insisted on driving again, and when they reached the Hayward Mansion, he opened her car door. She stood on the sidewalk, gazing up at the lights twinkling from the eaves, their reflections like little stars on the snow.

"It's beautiful," James said, coming to stand next to her.

They stood side by side, peacefully gazing at the house. Maggie sighed in contentment, and then forced herself to start up the walkway.

"I'll stay here unless you have someone to go home with you," James told her at the door.

"I can drive my car," she said.

"I know, but I'd like to know you're not alone. If someone volunteers to follow you home, I'll go ahead and walk to the station to pick up my car and you can drive yours."

"Thank you." She sincerely appreciated his thoughtfulness, but she hoped he wouldn't still be hovering over her tomorrow or it would be difficult to continue solving the mystery.

Before she could put her hand on the doorknob, Ruth pulled open the door and dragged Maggie inside. Ruth left the door ajar, so she'd undoubtedly seen James standing with her, but she ignored him and focused on Maggie.

Ruth ran her gaze up and down as if searching for something. "I should have known last night when you didn't show up at our meeting that you were in trouble. I should have come looking for you."

With the afternoon excitement, Maggie had all but forgotten about her evening in the cellar. She didn't really want to talk about it, but she wouldn't ignore her friend's kindness. "I'm all right, Ruth. I appreciate your concern."

"Concern, shoot." Ruth swept Maggie into a fierce hug. "How on earth did you survive the scare?"

Maggie didn't want to lose her good mood thinking about past terror, so she said, "With a warm jacket and my big mouth to yell for help."

Ruth pushed back and peered over her glasses, which were lodged near the end of her nose. "Well if you find yourself in need of looking at our records again, I'll be coming up to the attic with you, and I won't hear a bit of argument about it."

"I'd appreciate the company," Maggie said honestly. "I'd like to search for information on the chalice first thing in the morning. Are you available then?"

"I'll be at the historical society by nine. Will that work?"

"Perfect."

Ruth saw James over Maggie's shoulder. "I wasn't expecting you, James. Did you have something you needed to present at our meeting?"

James occasionally dropped in on the society's meetings, even though he wasn't a member. At Ruth's question, he pretended to shudder. "The horror!"

Maggie chuckled, but Ruth was unmoved, and Maggie stifled her merriment. "James insisted on driving me here."

"She needs to be more careful," James told Ruth. "I'd appreciate it if one of you would escort her home."

"You mean because of what happened last night?" Ruth asked.

"That and other things."

Ruth shot Maggie a look. "Did something else happen?"

"Nothing serious."

"The concern on James's face wouldn't be there from 'nothing serious.' You'll sit down and tell us all about it." Ruth latched onto Maggie's wrist and dragged her farther into the house. "We'll see that she gets home safely," Ruth called back to James.

Maggie cast a pleading look at James for his help in rescuing her from having to recount the story again, but a self-satisfied smirk appeared on his handsome face before he closed the door.

Maggie took a seat in the middle of the group and told them about the van that had followed her that afternoon and how this was the third time she'd seen it. She kept the telling short and tried to usher the conversation straight into the meeting, but Ruth interrupted.

"We can take turns being with you so you're not alone," she offered.

"That's not necessary," Maggie protested. "Especially since I don't even know if I'm in danger."

"Not in danger." Ina rolled her eyes. "Of course you are."

"No, really," Maggie replied. "The man hasn't shown any sign of wanting to harm me. He didn't come after me the first time I saw him, and I wasn't injured in the cellar incident. He didn't try to run me off the road or anything today—he actually slowed down so he wouldn't hit me."

"It wouldn't hurt for you to be extra careful, though." Liz chewed on her lower lip.

"I agree," Maggie said. "But I don't need a bodyguard."

"Seems you already have one." Daisy winked.

Maggie stifled a groan.

"By the way, I stopped at the supermarket and talked with the owner, Rodney," Liz said.

Maggie could have hugged her friend for the change of subject.

"Adele was a longtime customer," Liz continued. "When she stopped leaving the house, Rodney agreed to deliver her groceries. He'd get a weekly email from Adele with a list of items. Like everyone else, she wouldn't let him into the house, so he'd leave the box on the back porch. He never saw the nurse or Adele. He charged the groceries to her account, then sent her a monthly statement and got payment in the mail."

"So another dead end," Maggie said and the atmosphere in the room darkened. She didn't want to bring her friends down, so she lifted the shopping bag she'd brought. "I was able to make twenty punched-metal star ornaments this morning. How about everyone else?"

The women started discussing the tree, and Maggie exhaled slowly. She appreciated her newfound friends and would take their advice to heart, but she had to get to the bottom of this mystery.

The meeting didn't last much longer than it took to hang the ornaments and review the plans for each room. Maggie had nothing to report on the foyer other than the mercury vase, but she promised to wade through Aunt Evelyn's Christmas decorations and come up with a plan before their next meeting.

June followed Maggie home. As she trudged up the front steps, she realized the toll her day had taken on her energy level. She waved to June before she closed the door. She was glad to finally be home alone to decompress.

She scooped up Snickers and hugged his furry body close. "I'm glad to be home, boy. It's been quite a day."

She heard the loud rumble of a vehicle passing on the street, and her gaze shot to the window. Could it be the van again? Was the man back? She should have taken her friends' advice and not stayed home alone.

Should she call the police?

"And report what?" she asked herself. She held an invisible phone to her ear. "Hello, Officer Linton, I heard a vehicle on the road."

He would think I've lost it. And if she ever found herself in need of their response in the future, they might not take her seriously.

Until or unless she saw the van and driver lurking outside, she was on her own.

She released Snickers and double-checked the front door lock, then traveled around the first floor and confirmed the windows and other doors were locked too.

Each look out into the blackened night raised her fear, as she was certain she would see the van outside her home every time. She finally took refuge in her bedroom, where she locked the door. She gave herself a pep talk as she climbed into bed and prayed that she'd make it through the night without another scare.

14

With grit and determination, Maggie put yesterday's troubles behind her. She was eager to meet Ruth to begin additional research on the chalice. After a big breakfast of scrambled eggs and bacon, she left the Jetta at the manor and strolled down Shoreline Drive. As she walked, her boots whisked through fresh powdery flakes from a midnight snowfall, and the sun broke free from early morning clouds. Just a hint of salty spray tinged the air, but it grew stronger as she approached The Busy Bean, where outdoor speakers played *Jingle Bells*. She picked up the tune, humming along as she walked. She imagined a one-horse sleigh gliding through the snow as the song claimed.

As she spotted the church, her mood faltered. Thoughts of Old Faith Chapel usually brought calm, but today it reminded her of her evening in the cellar and put a pall on her morning.

"Ignore it," she warned herself and changed her focus to the school, where two elementary-age children were having a snowball fight on the playground. Their laughter rang out and helped her modify her attitude.

Farther down the road, she caught the sun's bright rays illuminating the historical society's Victorian. All thoughts fled her mind, and she simply enjoyed the crisp white snow that blanketed the yard, bringing depth to the Queen Anne's rose color while the sun electrified the teal trim. It was a breathtaking sight that would never get old, and she would have loved to stand and look at it, but she had a job to do.

She rushed up the steps and through the door, calling, "I'm here, Ruth."

Footsteps sounded on the building's original hardwood floor and Ruth popped around the corner.

"Right on time as usual. It's bound to be cold in the attic." Ruth shrugged into her jacket. "Before we get started, you should know I stopped at the pharmacy on the way over. Steve said Adele hadn't gotten prescriptions filled at his store in years."

"Why not?"

"He wouldn't go into details, just said they had a falling out about a prescription. She got so mad that she refused to set foot in his store."

"That's a bit extreme, isn't it?"

"Maybe for today's generation, but Adele's generation is different. They prefer to deal with their issues on their own and not talk about them. Steve might have needed to ask questions that she didn't want to answer, and she refused to do business with him after that."

"So we've struck out again," Maggie said.

"She had to get her prescriptions filled somewhere. She wasn't a healthy woman, especially later in life. We could check nearby towns."

Maggie doubted that tactic. "Since we don't know these pharmacists, chances are they won't give out any information."

"I can still do some checking for you," Ruth said as she started up the stairs.

Maggie thought about telling her not to bother, but Ruth was a doer. No matter what Maggie said, Ruth would continue to search.

In the attic, Maggie took a gander around as Ruth flicked on the light. The roof angled down on both sides. One wall was covered with handmade shelves holding boxes of records. The other side of the room was littered with old furniture. A small window facing the front allowed sunlight to filter in and highlight years of dust on the aged pine floorboards.

"I know this might sound strange," Ruth said from the middle of the room, "but I love coming up here. My grandmother had a similar attic, and I played in it with my cousins. We'd dig out all of her old clothes and shoes and imagine ourselves in a long-past time. Guess that's where I learned to love history so much."

"I had a similar experience with my aunt, but we didn't dress up. She told amazing stories about the old things she'd stored in her attic. A nineteenth-century carpet bag was my favorite because I knew it had seen so many adventures." Maggie paused to think. "I wonder if it's still up there."

"Wouldn't it be fun if you found it?" Ruth dragged a chair to a round table and sat.

Maggie settled onto a chair next to her and showed Ruth a picture of the chalice on her phone. "We're looking for anything about the chalice, and the key, of course. Plus anything to do with Deacon Arndt's arrival in town in the early 1700s. Keep your eyes open for items about the Kessler family too."

They flipped though folders holding fragile old documents, papers, and photos that the society had collected from the townspeople. After the holidays were over, they would organize and choose which items to display in their small museum, and then put the other items in quality archival storage. They often changed out the museum's displays to encourage locals to visit and promote the town's history.

Ruth flipped through pages and started humming a melody that Maggie knew but couldn't identify. After another restless night, the rhythmic sound soon made Maggie's eyes droop and her head lower.

"Got something!" Ruth exclaimed.

Maggie snapped up her head to see Ruth holding a yellowed document.

Ruth ran a finger along the printing and read silently. "I never knew this."

"What?" Maggie asked eagerly.

"Adele Kessler is a descendant of Deacon Arndt's family. This says that Lewis Kessler was Deacon Arndt's uncle, and he supported Arndt when he first came to America. In fact, he was instrumental in bringing the deacon to Somerset Harbor."

Maggie glanced at the paper. "Odd that no one has mentioned it."

"Not as odd as you might think." Ruth adjusted her glasses. "If every bit of history was retained over the years, there would be no need for a society like ours."

"Good point. This could confirm the connection between the key and the chalice."

"Then let's keep looking."

Maggie applied herself diligently, reading every kind of record imaginable. She doubted that many of the documents had real historical value, but they painted a good picture of the town's history.

Maggie soon located an old leather journal. She paused in a section that described the building of the church and had rough sketches of the building as it was erected. The author described a dedication ceremony, and there was a sketch of several men standing out front. It was dated November 1731.

"Look at this." Maggie held out the journal and explained the sequence. "Do you think the man in the black robe is Deacon Arndt?"

Ruth lifted her glasses and bent closer to consider the drawing. "Likely, I suppose. Turn the page."

The next page was an intricate sketch of the chalice.

"The jewels are all in the right places," Ruth said in awe.

Maggie nearly jumped out of her skin, but she contained her excitement. "So the chalice is real, and Deacon Arndt most likely brought it to this country." She flipped through the journal, hoping to spot something about the key too, but neither of them found any additional information in the journal or in the rest of the archives.

Maggie tapped the drawing of Arndt. "I suppose you don't want me to take the journal with me."

"Sorry, but I don't like to let anything leave the building. Not that I don't trust you, but bad things can happen even with your best efforts."

"I understand." Maggie used her phone to take several pictures of the journal and its pages in case she needed them. "Thank you for working on this with me."

"Work?" Ruth winked. "Looking at these old items is fun for me."

"It would be a whole lot more fun if I knew for sure a woman wasn't in danger."

Ruth patted her shoulder. "You'll figure it out. I know you will."

Maggie wished she could be so certain.

She bid Ruth goodbye, then strolled to Carriage House Antiques. The sun shone down on her, but she barely noticed it as she puzzled over what could have happened to the chalice. She was so intent she passed the shop and had to retrace her steps.

She pushed open the door just as June appeared out of the workroom, carrying a large mug of tea. "You're back early. I hope that doesn't mean you didn't find anything."

"On the contrary." Maggie was relaying her discovery when a sudden thought hit her. "Maybe we're looking at this all wrong."

"How's that?" June hoisted herself onto a stool.

Maggie perched on the stool on the other side of the counter. "The connection between the chalice and Adele's family has me wondering if *she* was behind its theft."

June choked on her tea. "How could you say that?"

"I didn't mean Adele actually stole it, but what if she believed the chalice should belong to her family due to her relation to Deacon Arndt? She might have asked for it and the church refused. So Chad, who by this time was a real little criminal, nabbed it. Or Adele could have hired someone else to steal it."

June's face creased in a pensive expression. "I suppose that's more plausible, but still it's pretty far-fetched."

"Yes, but if so, the key could lead to the chalice's location. Perhaps Adele hid the chalice and never told Chad where it was. He would have been desperate to find it because he knew what it was worth, so he kidnapped the woman who hid the key."

"I don't know," June said hesitantly. "Still sounds like a crazy theory."

Maggie grabbed June's hand. "Think about it. Perhaps the money was gone long before Adele took to her bed. The state of the house certainly suggests they'd run out of money."

"But what about the antiques you saw in the catalog? Surely Adele would have sold those, not stolen from her church."

"You know the last thing many of these older families do is to part with family possessions. They see themselves as caretakers of the heirlooms—selling them is a betrayal."

"But the chalice belonged to the family too, so why would she have been willing to sell it?"

"I don't know. Possibly because she didn't see the chalice when she was growing up?"

"You could be right, I suppose." June lifted her mug and sipped. "The first thing we need to know is the value of the chalice. If the jewels weren't real, it wouldn't be worth stealing or selling."

"You're great at valuing items. Could you contact your sources and try to get an estimate for the chalice without jewels, and I'll check with my jeweler to get an estimate on the jewels?"

June's eyes lit up. "I'm all over it."

The door opened, and James stepped inside with a rush of chilly air.

He peered first at Maggie, then at June and back again. "You two look as thick as thieves."

"I was just going to the office to do some work." June grabbed her mug and disappeared.

James rounded on Maggie. "Well?"

Maggie recounted her discovery and their plan. "Do you think Chad could have stolen the chalice?"

James shrugged as he took the seat June had vacated. "He was a suspect back then, but he had a strong alibi. I never knew what it was, but the police chief at the time was content with it." He leaned his elbows on the counter. "After what I've learned about Chad today, though, I doubt the Kesslers needed money."

Maggie was on the edge of her stool. "What?"

"I located Chad's address in Portland. He was living in a small apartment, but he recently bought a huge estate. Online property records show he didn't take out a mortgage—he paid cash."

"Adele's money?"

"I suspect so. He's a waiter. Not the kind of job where he'd have the money for a big house. Adele must have left him a large inheritance."

Maggie's shoulders dropped. "That would negate my theory of the family having run out of money."

"That's true, but it opens up a whole new theory. If Chad needed or wanted his mother's money sooner, he could have killed her, and everything else that has happened is related somehow."

Maggie's hand flew to her chest. "You think he's capable of murdering his own mother?"

"I wouldn't like to think so, but people do crazy things for money."

Maggie shot to her feet. "We have to find Adele's cause of death, and we need to find it now."

"Slow down," he said, laying a hand on her arm. "We have to go through proper channels if we want to get to the truth. I have a few contacts that might be able to give me that information."

"Perfect. Thank you." She grabbed a notepad and pen. "I'll need Chad's address."

"What for?" James asked, and then shook his head. "Why'd I even ask? You're planning to go see him." It wasn't a question.

"Of course. It's vital now."

James's brows creased in a deep furrow. "You're not going alone."

Maggie began to protest, but then thoughts of Chad killing his mother popped into her head. Facing a potential killer alone would be foolish. She might be impulsive when she was solving a mystery, but she wasn't stupid. "I'd be glad to have the company."

"I won't be free until about three. I'll pick you up here, okay?"

"I'll be ready."

"If I'm lucky, you'll have calmed down by then." He grinned at her.

"Don't hold your breath. Waiting will only get me more stirred up, so I'll be ready to put Chad through his paces." She pretended to twist the end of a fake mustache.

He shook his head and got up to leave. "Never a dull moment with you, Maggie Watson."

"Is that a good thing?"

"I'm not sure." He paused at the door and looked back at her. "I'll let you know at three."

When he was gone, Maggie emailed a copy of the chalice's photo to Nigel Holman, asking him to call her. Five minutes later, her phone rang.

"Please tell me you have the real chalice for me to look at," he said. He sounded like he might try to climb through the phone if she did.

"Sorry. Just a picture."

"You tease."

"I know this is a crazy request, but I wondered—if we assume the jewels are real and are of the same quality as the ones found in the key, could you give me a ballpark estimate of the chalice's value?"

"Your request isn't ridiculous, actually, but there's one thing you're forgetting. We know they used real stones in the key, but because the chalice is so large, they could have used imitations."

Maggie's excitement dropped a notch. "I suppose, but we believe this chalice was a gift from a very wealthy family so I'd bet they're real."

"In that case, let me take a little time to work on a very loose estimate, and I'll get back to you."

"Thank you, Nigel."

"Please remember, anything I tell you is pure supposition."

"Of course," she said, and they hung up.

She spent the next hour helping a couple from out of town select the perfect piece as a wedding present for their only granddaughter. They settled on an entire set of Royal Standard bone china in a darling pattern with a white background and delicate purple pansies, and Maggie could almost see the joy on their granddaughter's face.

After arranging delivery, she bid the couple goodbye and sat down to check her phone. No missed calls or emails from Nigel. *What is taking him so long?*

The back door opened and June hurried toward Maggie, her face alight with excitement. "I just talked to my expert, and boy, have I got news for you! Assuming the chalice is made of real silver and the etching is real gold, it would be worth around $10,000 in today's market."

Maggie hadn't expected it to fetch such a high dollar amount without the jewels. "Okay, so it's even more valuable than I thought and definitely something worth stealing."

"Especially if the jewels are real."

"Especially then."

"I have bonus info for you too." Her eyes were bright with anticipation.

Maggie pointed an accusatory finger. "You love sleuthing as much as I do."

"Most people who collect antiques do, don't they? We all want to find the story behind our treasures."

"That's true. What's your other news?"

June took a seat across the counter from Maggie. "Several of the dealers I spoke with told me that Chad has been selling off the family antiques for the past two years. He's hit most every antiques shop in the state. Looks like he's trying to keep the proprietors from knowing he was selling a large number of his mother's items."

"So he needed money. Or wanted it. Question is, did his mother know he was doing it?"

"Wouldn't she miss the items?"

"If she was bedridden, she'd never know."

June shook her head in disgust. "I guess I wouldn't put it past the Chad I've heard stories about. Poor Adele. But you know, I was thinking about her in the office. She continued to give a generous donation to the historical society every year. That would suggest she wasn't destitute, right?"

"Perhaps not. Or perhaps she was selling antiques so she had the money to continue her donations," Maggie surmised. "One thing is becoming clearer to me—only Chad can answer these questions."

Her phone chimed, indicating a new email. She glanced at the screen. "It's from Nigel."

"Hurry up and read it." June leaned closer.

Maggie opened the email and quickly scanned the message. She sat back, speechless.

"What?" June clutched Maggie's arm.

"If the jewels are real and the same quality as the ones in the key, Nigel thinks the chalice's value would be in the $100,000 range."

June leaned back and let out a rush of breath. "That's a lot of money."

Maggie thoughtfully tapped her chin with a finger. "Definitely enough money to make kidnapping a viable option. Even enough for a son to commit murder."

15

Maggie and James drove into the classy Portland neighborhood that was home to Chad's large two-story house overlooking the ocean. Set on a hill, the contemporary building had elaborate angles and rooflines, a stone façade, blue siding, and tall windows. The landscaping was buried under snow, but modern sculptures and sleek planters peeked above the snowline.

James parked on the street out front, and Maggie stared up at the place as she climbed out. "It'd take big bucks to afford a place like this."

"It goes for close to a million." James started up the walkway, and Maggie followed.

The front door was made of expensive African ebony. "You're sure there's no way Chad could have saved his money?"

James rolled his eyes.

"Granted, waiters aren't well paid, but you never know. He could be a smart investor."

"Even with investments, I doubt he could swing this place. He'd have to win a lottery."

"That's a possibility." Maggie rang the doorbell and she heard it chime from inside the home.

James shook his head. "If he'd won the lottery, the news would have spread through Somerset Harbor like wildfire."

The doorknob twisted, and Maggie's attention locked on the door. She was finally going to meet the infamous Chad, and she planned to thoroughly assess him from the moment he appeared.

The door opened, and he stood for a moment, staring at them from beneath bushy black eyebrows and closely cropped hair. He had a medium build and wore a New England Patriots sweatshirt with dark jeans.

"Hi, Chad." James sounded confident, but Maggie could see hesitation in his expression.

Confusion flickered across Chad's face before recognition dawned. "Do I know . . . hey, it's you! James! From Somerset Harbor. We dug up Mom's rosebush. How the heck are you?" Chad reached out to shake James's hand and pumped enthusiastically.

Maggie hadn't expected such a warm welcome, but then Chad didn't know the reason for their visit.

"Where are the manners my mother drilled into me?" Chad stepped aside. "Come on in."

James introduced Maggie as they crossed the threshold into a soaring foyer. She could see straight through the house to a bank of windows on the far side of the building. Moving boxes cluttered a front room with an expensive chandelier hanging from the ceiling; Maggie assumed it was supposed to be a dining room.

"Don't mind the mess," Chad called over his shoulder as he took off for the back of the house. "I just moved in."

They entered the family room with high ceilings and windows. The furniture was dark, sparse, and well worn, exactly what she might expect from a bachelor who worked as a waiter.

Chad grimaced, his full lips narrowing. "Wish you'd waited a few weeks for my new furniture to arrive and my decorator to get this place in shape." He gestured at the sofa. "But have a seat and I'll grab some drinks."

He didn't bother to ask what they wanted but disappeared into the attached kitchen with white cabinets and granite countertops.

Maggie sat next to James on the sofa and kept her voice low. "New house. New furniture. A decorator."

"All require money," James noted quietly.

Chad returned with an assortment of fancy bottles of infused water. He set them on the glass coffee table and dropped to the floor. "Help yourselves."

"Thanks." James took a lemon flavor, which hissed as he twisted off the cap. Maggie chose a raspberry-flavored water, but she didn't open it.

"So, hey, man." Chad twisted open a cherry drink and took a long swig. "What brings you here?"

"I bought a vase at your mother's estate sale," Maggie began.

"Let me guess. You discovered it was junk and you want your money back." Chad grinned.

Maggie couldn't laugh at the joke of a man she suspected had done terrible things, so she gave him a weak smile instead. "I was surprised and sad to see your mother's house in such disrepair."

Chad's face fell. "Yeah, man, that was a bad deal."

"What happened?" James asked.

Chad stared at James. A hard edge came into his eyes, but then he lightened up and shrugged. "I don't much like your question, but I guess people in Somerset Harbor are bound to gossip about it. Might as well tell you so they at least get it right."

"Don't worry, we don't plan to share anything you tell us," James said.

"Good to hear, but I know there's gossip out there already, and you can do me a favor by stopping it. Or at least getting the facts straight." He took another long pull on his bottle. "Mom hired a shady contractor who took her for big bucks. She was embarrassed that she got taken, and she became suspicious of everyone outside of the family—so everyone but me and my cousins, Sarah and Abby." He set his bottle on the table and fiddled with it.

"I remember your cousins. They still live around here?" James's tone sounded harmless enough, but Maggie knew he was fishing.

"Sarah's in Pelican Cove and Abby's right here in Portland."

"I'd like to look them up too. Could I get their phone numbers?"

Chad arched a brow and considered James for a moment, but he dug out his phone and rattled off the numbers so James could tap them into his phone's address book.

"You were saying about your mother," Maggie prompted.

Chad set his water down. "When I saw the house, I arranged to have workers come out, but Mom wouldn't let them near the place. I tried to get her to see that things were falling apart, but she said she'd rather it fall down around her than have 'charlatans' working on it again." He rolled his eyes. "Her word, not mine."

"Why did she disappear?" James asked. "She was always so involved, but then suddenly no one was seeing her."

Chad scooted back on the rug and chewed on the inside of his cheek.

"Remember, we're not going to tell anyone else." James sounded polite, but Maggie detected an edge in his tone.

"She got feeble, you know. Old age and stuff." Chad returned to playing with his drink and Maggie sensed a lie coming. "She couldn't take care of herself. Stopped going out and didn't want to see anyone. If you ask me, she didn't trust anyone anymore. Or she was too embarrassed over getting taken in the scam. I actually don't know why she did the whole hermit thing, but when she started to get sick, I used my trust fund allowance to hire a live-in nurse to take care of her. She was furious." He tried to chuckle, but it sounded sad. "Said I was taking away her independence."

"No one in town seems to have met this nurse," Maggie said. "What's her name?"

Chad's head popped up and so did his eyebrows. "Why do you want to know?"

"Just curious," Maggie responded.

"I'd rather not get her involved. You know how Somerset Harbor gossip is. They'll say she scammed Mom or killed her or something within the week. I need to consider her privacy."

"If I came to you and asked for a reference for someone to care for my mom, I'm sure you'd be happy to share the nurse's contact information," James pressed.

"But that's not what you're asking, is it?" Chad's voice hardened.

"No, and it really doesn't matter," James said lightly. "We were just wondering."

"Gotcha." Chad didn't sound convinced.

Maggie recognized it was time to change the subject. "I ran into the curator at your estate sale. Funny thing. I was talking to him, and he didn't even know you existed."

Chad stared at his crisscrossed legs. "Mom wanted everything handled through her executor and attorneys. She was still mad about the nurse. I thought she was going to disinherit me."

"Your mother must have had a large estate. You probably inherited a lot of money," Maggie said in a musing tone. *I'm really pushing it now.*

Chad's head slowly came up, and if looks could kill, Maggie and James would have been dead on the floor. "Is that what this is about? You're some of the people who want some of my money? 'Cause if you are," he jumped to his feet, "you should leave."

"No, we don't want money," James said quickly. "We—"

"You know what, I don't care. I don't like these questions." He gestured at the front door. "The gossips in that stupid town can say what they want. I want you to leave."

He charged out of the room. Maggie hadn't had a chance to ask all the questions burning in her brain, so she ran after him.

"The family antiques you've been selling off for the last

two years," she called out. "Were the proceeds for you, or did your mother direct you to sell them?"

He spun on her, anger blazing in his eyes. "I didn't sell anything. I wouldn't ever part with family heirlooms, even that ramshackle old house."

He must be outright lying now, but they were almost at the door, and Maggie had to ask about the chalice. "Did you steal the chalice?"

"Really? You're gonna bring that up too?" He yanked open the door and glared at her. "I don't know who you think you are, lady, but you're not welcome here." James put himself between them, and Chad turned on him. "And you, man. We were friends once. This was a pretty low thing to do."

"I didn't mean it to be," James said. "We came for the truth."

"Truth about what? That I got money from my mom? Yeah. I did. Lots of it. Now get lost."

Maggie and James traded a look. What else could they do? They stepped outside and the door slammed behind them.

"Wow. He's hiding something," James said as they walked quickly down the sidewalk toward the car. "That was perfectly clear."

"Question is, what is he hiding? And did it involve murdering his mother?"

James opened her door for her. She couldn't read his expression. He jogged around the front of the car and climbed in, then started the car and gave her a look. "Do you honestly think Chad killed his mother?"

"I don't know. What about you?"

"It's hard to imagine someone you played with as a kid is a murderer, you know?"

"I suppose it is."

"When we get back to town, I'll check on Sarah and Abby." Seeming lost in his thoughts, James got the car on the road.

Maggie settled into the leather seat, her thoughts going to Chad. She was going over the conversation in her head when her phone rang.

"It's June. Maybe she's located something important for us." Maggie answered the call.

"Are you back in town yet?" June asked.

"We're on the way home now."

"Okay . . . well, I was hoping to tell you about this in person, but I've got plans tonight, so I'll give it to you now. I did some additional research on chalices bestowed on deacons at their ordinations."

"Mind if I put you on speaker so James can hear?"

June agreed and Maggie pressed the speaker button.

"So . . ." June started. "Not that I didn't believe Pastor David when he said a jeweled chalice was too expensive for a church to purchase, especially back in the day, but . . ." She took a long breath. "I've confirmed his assumption. There's no way the church purchased it."

"It's good to know he was right." Maggie tried to hide her disappointment at such lackluster news. *This doesn't help much.* "I appreciate your doing the research."

"Don't sound so disappointed." June chuckled. "That's not the news I called about. I investigated Deacon Arndt's history on a genealogy website I belong to."

"And?"

"And I located information on the site about his family, and then emailed several people from his family tree. One of them confirmed that a rich ancestor gave the chalice to the deacon."

"Oh, good. I'm glad we know that's certain too." *Unfortunately, this doesn't move our investigation forward, either.*

"Again, this isn't the good part."

Maggie waited for June to go on, but silence filled the phone. She glanced at James. He shrugged.

"Okay, I'll bite," Maggie finally said when the silence got to her. "What's the good part?"

"In the email, the guy said the chalice was housed in a decorative wooden box." She paused again.

"And?" Maggie demanded.

"And the box was fastened with an ornate lock with two jewels."

"Oh my gosh, the key!" Maggie cried. "The jeweled key could be for the chalice box!"

"Bingo!" June exclaimed.

"The box wouldn't be huge," James said. "Wouldn't the key be too big for it?"

He might be right, but she wanted to savor a victory for a moment. "I prefer to think the key fits the box and it might contain something that can help us solve the mystery."

"I agree," June said. "Do you remember a box in the catalog of items for Adele's auction?"

"I didn't see one," Maggie said. "James?"

He shook his head. "What next, then?"

"Next?" Maggie stared at him; her direction was clear. "Next I pull out all the stops to find this box."

16

With each step to Carriage House Antiques the next morning, Maggie's curiosity rose. June had phoned a few minutes after eight insisting she needed Maggie at the shop immediately. Maggie hadn't even had breakfast, but something in June's tone had told her that forgoing breakfast would be worth it.

She rounded the corner, and June whipped open the front door. "Come on!" She nearly danced on the balls of her feet and gestured for Maggie to hurry. As soon as Maggie was within arm's reach, June grabbed her hand and dragged her inside. "I can't wait to show you."

"You could just tell me what you have," Maggie said as June tugged her down the narrow shop aisle.

"Seeing is so much better." June towed Maggie all the way to the back office, where she had a picture up on the computer.

A photo of an open wooden chest filled the screen. Purple velvet lined the box, which was about the size of a very thick briefcase. It held a jeweled chalice along with several other pieces crafted specifically for serving communion.

"That's Deacon Arndt's chalice!"

"That's not all." June opened another photo, which showed the closed box. There was a jewel-encrusted lock on the front of it. Inserted in the lock was a key identical to the one Maggie had discovered in the vase, though it had no compass.

Maggie's gaze shot up. "The key does fit this box."

June's self-satisfied expression said it all.

"Yes!" Maggie raised her hands. "We finally know what the key is for!"

June dropped into the chair and her joy disappeared. "Unfortunately I haven't come up with any ideas on where the box might be located."

Maggie took a closer look at the box. "How did you find the pictures?"

"I was emailing back and forth with Arndt's family. One of them described the pictures she had, so I had her scan and send them."

"Okay." Maggie's mind raced to process the new information. At long last, they were finally getting closer to helping the note writer. "Now it's even more important that we find the chest."

June pointed at the screen. "Note that this key doesn't have the compass attached."

Maggie glanced at the picture then back at June. "You think the compass is a clue to finding the box?"

"I do, and my best guess is that either Chad has it, or Adele hid it somewhere away from her property. If she hid it on her property, then whoever might be holding the woman captive could have found it, which meant the woman wouldn't have had to write the note in the first place."

"Can you keep searching online for more leads?" Maggie asked.

"Um . . ." June stretched her arms. "I've actually been here all night working on this."

Maggie took a good look at her friend. She had dark circles under her eyes and was wearing the same clothes as yesterday. "You're a real trouper, June, and I appreciate you more each day."

June blushed and waved off the praise. "Any thoughts on how to find this box other than an online search?"

"I think Adele is the key—no pun intended." Maggie wrinkled her nose. "We know the deacon brought the chalice to Somerset Harbor, so we can guess the chest and key came with him. If we do more research on Adele, we may find out if she ever had the box, and if so, where she might have hidden it."

"Well, then." June's enthusiasm reignited in her eyes. "A trip to The Busy Bean is in order. It's bound to be packed with people who knew Adele."

Maggie stood. "I know you were up all night, but do you mind watching the shop so I can talk to them? We're so close, and I need to help that woman as soon as possible. It's been a week!"

"I'm good as long as we don't run out of coffee." June lifted her mug.

Maggie gave June a quick hug, and then raced out of the shop and down the street to The Busy Bean. Usually she took the time to admire the shoreline as she walked, but she was sure the solution to the mystery was right around the corner, and she wouldn't let anything distract her.

Maggie waved to Daisy as she scoped out the shop. Her gaze landed on Liz, who leaned against the takeout counter. Maggie made a beeline toward her friend.

"You look like a woman on a mission." Liz pulled money from her wallet to pay the cashier.

"I am." Maggie quickly filled her in. "So can you share anything you know about Adele?"

Liz's expression faded into seriousness. "I didn't know her well, but I do know she served on the church's altar guild for many years. Come rain or shine, she prepared the church altar and pulpit every week with linens she personally cleaned."

"Guess she had the same love for the church as Deacon Arndt."

Liz settled her change into her wallet. "She was so fanatical about the job. I often thought the altar and pulpit held personal meaning for her and that's why she was so devoted to taking care of them. Knowing Arndt was a member of her family—that makes more sense."

Maggie let her imagination wander to the church, and she could see Adele stripping the altar cloths, polishing the oak, and then placing newly pressed cloths carefully back over it. "You don't think . . . no, that's too crazy."

"Think what?" Liz asked.

Maggie shook her head.

"C'mon, think what?" Liz prodded. "You can't shut me out now, Maggie, especially if it involves the church."

Maggie leaned closer so no one could overhear them. "What if there's a hidden compartment in the altar or pulpit, and Adele hid the chalice and chest there? Since she took care of the altar and the pulpit, no one, not even the pastor, would think to look there."

Liz's expression perked up. "That's not crazy. In fact, it makes perfect sense. As the church founder, Deacon Arndt likely designed both pieces. If he wanted to be sure his expensive communion service was hidden and safe, a secret compartment would be logical."

Maggie grabbed Liz's arm. "We have to check."

"I'm with you on that one."

Liz faced the counter. "Can I get my coffee now, Daisy?"

Daisy prepared the to-go cup, but she held it out of Liz's reach. "If you want your caffeine fix, you're going to have to tell me what's going on."

"If our theory proves true, and if it's something I can share, I'll come back and tell you," Maggie promised.

"Okay, fine." Daisy surrendered the cup. "Take the coffee. You paid for it after all."

Liz grabbed the cup before Daisy could change her mind.

"You better come back here soon." Daisy's lips dipped in a pout that Maggie had seen her use on Harry with great effect, but Maggie and Liz were immune to Daisy's charms.

Maggie darted for the door before Daisy got even more curious and blocked the way.

Maggie and Liz raced toward Old Faith Chapel. The wind howled, preventing conversation, so Maggie put her head down and focused on getting to the church. As they reached the antique double wood door, a thought sprouted in her mind. She dug the jeweled key out of her bag.

Liz held the door. "If you're getting out the key, you must really think you're going to find the box."

"I just had another thought." Maggie stood in the doorway and held out the compass. The needle spun and landed due north, pointing toward the front of the church. Maggie showed the compass to Liz.

"You think the fact that this is pointing north was Adele's way to hint at the box's location?" Liz sounded dubious.

"Don't you?" Maggie asked. "You know, X marks the spot and all that."

"One way to find out." Liz led the way down the aisle.

Maggie's senses were hyperaware of everything—their footsteps ringing to the rafters, every creak of the building as the wind blasted into the old wood, the shift of the light on the pews as clouds obscured the sun.

Liz approached the front of the pulpit. "I think the deacon would be more likely to hide it here rather than the altar, since altars are sacred. Plus, more people approach the altar for various events, but very few have a reason to go into the pulpit."

"Agreed," Maggie said.

They climbed wide wooden stairs, and Liz carefully lifted the white linen extending over the podium. Maggie used her phone's flashlight to search the wood for a seam. The oak gleamed under the beam, but the wood was solid. She ran her hands over the lower portion with the same result and moved on to three built-in shelves under the podium.

"Hold my light." Maggie handed her phone to Liz and

squatted down. She ran her fingers over every inch of the shelves. She discovered a few books, a Bible, and breath mints, which she held up for Liz with a questioning look.

"David gets dry mouth sometimes," Liz said with a shrug.

"Like when his sermons are extra long?" Maggie winked.

Liz sighed. "He can get long-winded. He says the Spirit takes him and there's nothing he can do."

Maggie finished her inspection and sat back on her haunches. "I was sure we'd find a compartment hidden in the shelves."

Liz sulked. "Me too."

Maggie put her mind to work. "We didn't check the outside frame. It doesn't make as much sense, but it's possible."

Liz tugged Maggie to her feet. "It has to be there."

Maggie gazed out over the pews. "I've never been up here. David can really see everything that's going on, can't he?"

"Everything," Liz said with a note of humor in her voice.

Maggie vowed to fidget less in church from now on. She climbed down the stairs and approached the front of the pulpit. She ran her hands over the wood. "Liz, I've got two seams here!"

Excitement built in her stomach as she pressed on the edges, fully expecting the front section to pop up and reveal a hidden compartment. But nothing happened.

"I'm not surprised," Liz said as she peered down at Maggie. "If it were that easy to open, someone would have found it long ago."

"Okay, so there has to be a lever or a button to make it open." Maggie ran her flashlight over the gleaming wood.

"Could be the cross." She tried to slide the carved wood, then tried to twist it, and finally pressed and pulled.

Nothing.

Maggie stomped her foot in frustration, lost her balance, and grabbed the edge of the pulpit to right herself. The wood trim gave way. She teetered for a moment then fell to the hardwood floor.

"You're brilliant!" Liz cried out. "You found it."

"Right. Brilliant," Maggie scoffed as she got to her feet. But she saw that the panels had shifted a fraction of an inch, and she forgot all about her aching bottom. She grabbed a section and pulled it open as Liz raced down from the pulpit to join her. On a deep shelf, way in the back, there was a wooden box.

"Am I really seeing the chest?" she asked Liz, her voice hushed. "Or am I imagining it because I want to see it so badly?"

"It's real. Very real." Liz squeezed Maggie's hand. "Let's take it to David's office and open it."

Maggie carefully removed the box and admired the solid mahogany with its inlaid pearl top and a heart-shaped lock on the front. "It's heavy."

"The things that were well made are the only things that have lasted," Liz said as she headed for the office at a brisk pace.

Maggie nearly had to run to keep up. In David's office, Maggie set the box on his desk.

Liz locked the door behind them. "Don't want any prying eyes, do we?"

Maggie took the key from her pocket and inserted it in the lock.

"Here goes." She held her breath and twisted the key. There was a small *click*, and the catch released.

"It worked!" Liz wiggled with anticipation. "Open it."

Maggie lifted the lid and stood back in amazement. Purple velvet lined divided compartments, just as she'd seen in the picture. The largest compartment was empty, but the others held a hinged silver dish, a silver-topped faceted glass wine bottle, a silver spoon with a cross on the end, and a silver plate.

Maggie touched the empty slot, disappointment welling. "For the chalice."

"So it really was stolen."

"Looks like it." Maggie pored over each piece in silence, then closed and locked the box. "I suspect the box and serving pieces are valuable, but not nearly as much without the jeweled chalice."

"Do you think this box is what the woman was referring to when she said he was looking for the money?"

Maggie thought of the note, picturing the woman's last plea. *He said he loved me, but it's the money he loves. Please help. He'll kill me if we don't find what it opens. He's coming. Hurry!*

Maggie stared at the box, willing it to tell her how to find the woman. "This could be sold for cash, and with the chalice it would fetch over $100,000. So, yeah. I think it could be." A clock mentally ticked down in her head, and she still had no idea how much time was left, if any. "I'm not sure what we should do now. We don't even know who this belongs to. It could be considered church property or it could belong to Adele."

"We should get David's take on it. He's out of town for the day, so we'd better store it somewhere safe until he gets home." Liz glanced around, as if searching for a place to hide it. "Should we put it back in the pulpit? It's been safe there for who knows how long."

"Sure. Why not?" Maggie picked up the box.

Liz went to the door. Maggie grabbed the key from the desk, but fumbled it and it clanked to the floor. She bent to retrieve it . . . and heard something jingle in the box. She gently tilted it the other way. "Did you hear that?"

"Something's loose in there."

Maggie set the box back on the table and reopened it. All the communion pieces were firmly nestled in place. She picked up one end and listened.

"It's coming from the bottom." She started removing the items then felt around the edge of the velvet. She found a gap and lifted out the compartments.

"A false bottom," she muttered as she ran her fingers along the wood beneath the compartments. She continued to slide her fingers millimeter after millimeter until she found a difference in the wood and pressed.

The wood popped up, and Maggie lifted it out.

"Oh my." The words barely made it out of Maggie's mouth. *I would never have imagined finding this. Not in my wildest dreams.*

An untold fortune in jewels of sparkling reds, greens, and blues lay on black velvet in the bottom of the chest. There was also antique jewelry—gold and silver bracelets, brooches, necklaces, rings, and a strand of pearls.

Maggie and Liz alternated between gaping at the jewels and each other. Words failed them both and silence hung in the air.

Maggie remembered the woman whose life they were trying to save and shook herself. She carefully pulled out several pieces to examine them. All were antique. All showcased magnificent precious stones, and she suspected all of them were real and worth vast amounts of money.

She met Liz's gaze. "This is what the man in the note was looking for."

"Yes." Liz dropped into a chair. "I can't even begin to imagine how much the jewelry is worth. Why would Adele hide it here?"

"When Chad started getting into trouble, she could have been afraid he would steal it."

"Could be. It's sad that a mother might have had to take precautions like that against her own son."

Maggie couldn't think about that now. "You know what this means, don't you? It makes the note far more plausible and a woman could very well be in danger."

He'll kill me if we don't find what it opens. He's coming. Hurry! The words echoed through Maggie's mind. A week had passed since she'd found the note, and the pressure to locate this woman filled Maggie with new urgency.

Liz took a deep breath. "One thing's certain. She's not being held at the Kessler estate. On my way into town, I saw a For Sale sign on the property. Surely, a woman wouldn't be held prisoner in a house when it was for sale. That would draw too much unwanted attention."

"You may be right." Maggie had settled the jewels back in the box when a thought captivated her mind. "But if Chad put the house up for sale, he couldn't be involved in the abduction."

"Which means a potential buyer could accidently stumble upon the man and woman hiding there." Liz shuddered. "If she thinks he'd kill for this, it could put someone else's life in danger too."

"We can't let that happen." Maggie pulled her shoulders back. "I've been patient enough. I've got to get into that house."

"I know the realtor who listed the house. I'll call her and ask her to show it to us." Liz scurried to the desk phone and dialed.

Maggie stared at the jewels and let the day's events filter through her mind. "There's something off about all of this, Liz. Yesterday Chad said that he'd never sell the house."

"Oh. That *is* curious."

"Then again, he also said he'd never sell the family antiques, but I know that's not true. Maybe he's been lying to us about everything. If the woman isn't being held at the Kessler house, he could be involved in the kidnapping after all. Wouldn't surprise me. He wasn't a very nice man. He could have even . . ." Maggie wanted to add that he could have killed his mother too, but Liz held up a finger as she started talking to the realtor.

"Hey, Karen, it's Liz . . . I'm doing well . . ." Liz signaled Maggie to calm down; she was bouncing on her toes with impatience. "Well, I was wondering if you could show my friend Maggie and me the old Kessler place . . . Yeah, the one you just listed . . . Could you meet us there as soon as possible? We've got some free time,"

Liz said, clearly making a great effort to stay casual. "That would be perfect. See you soon."

As soon as Liz hung up, Maggie tugged her friend to her feet. "Road trip?"

"After we stow the valuables. I'll go out in the hall to make sure no one is around to see us. You wait at the door until I tell you. I feel like a real detective."

"Me too."

Liz ducked from the room, and Maggie repacked and locked the box before poking her head out the door. Liz soon waved from the end of the hallway, and Maggie rushed to join her.

They made quick work of stowing the box back in the pulpit and ran to pick up Liz's vehicle at The Busy Bean. As they drove to the Kessler estate, Maggie's thoughts raced as fast as the engine.

They found realtor Karen Newton standing on the tumbledown porch, the door open behind her. She was short and wide with vivid red hair and a ready smile. Liz introduced Maggie as they entered the dining room. The place had been cleared after the estate sale, revealing stained and tattered paisley wallpaper, and making the place feel even more dismal.

Liz slowly revolved in the center of the room, her eyes sad. "It's awful to see how the house has fallen on hard times. It must have been an amazing place in its day."

Karen planted hands on very generous hips and clicked her tongue. "I don't know how the owners could have let this lovely home go to ruin."

"If you don't mind my asking, who listed the property with you?" Maggie asked Karen.

A stern expression settled on her round face.

"That's okay," Maggie said. "I didn't mean to pry. I talked to Adele's son, Chad, yesterday, and he said he'd never sell the house. I guess he must have had a change of mind."

"Yesterday?" Karen arched a brow. "He listed the house last week, but asked me to wait until after the estate sale to post the listing."

So Chad did lie to us. Maggie should have felt satisfied that she was right about his character, but she felt sick to her stomach at his deception. *What if he is also capable of kidnapping an innocent woman and murdering his own mother?*

"I'd like to tour the entire home if I may," Maggie said.

"No problem. You two go ahead without me. I have a few phone calls to make. Take your time."

Maggie immediately led Liz up the stairs. On the upper landing, she leaned close to her friend and lowered her voice. "With the estate sale, the woman wouldn't have been held on the first floor, so I want to start up here. She could be in the attic or a hidden room."

Maggie went straight to the door at the far end of the hall, where she guessed the attic was, and reached for the doorknob.

Liz clutched the back of Maggie's shirt to stop her. "What if we actually find someone? Like the kidnapper? How are we going to protect ourselves?"

Maggie rummaged in her tote and pulled out a can of pepper spray.

Liz frowned. "I don't even want to know why you have that."

"Good. I don't want to tell you." Maggie pulled open the door and discovered the attic stairs.

They crept as silently as they could up centuries-old risers that squeaked each time they took a step. The room was windowless, dark, and spooky. Maggie waited for her eyes to adjust and listened. She heard no sounds and saw no movement.

Liz came up beside her and clutched her arm. "Now what?"

What indeed?

"Hello?" Maggie called out.

No response.

"We need light," Liz said quietly.

Maggie fished out her phone and shone its flashlight over the area. She spotted a cord dangling in the middle of the attic. She made her way over the wide plank floors and pulled it, turning on the light bulb it hung from. It took a moment for her eyes to adjust again, but when they did, frustration surfaced.

"Not a thing up here," Liz said, mirroring Maggie's thoughts.

"Chad's selling the house, so I guess it's not surprising."

Liz pointed at the floor a few feet ahead. "Looks like something's been dragged through the dust."

Two trails about the width of a pair of feet ran from the far wall to the stairway. They were solid lines, not separate footprints like the ones Maggie and Liz were leaving.

A bad feeling settled in Maggie's stomach. "Could be a person's shoes. Perhaps the woman was held captive up here, and then dragged to the door and out when the house was listed."

"Or perhaps she was dead." Liz put voice to thoughts Maggie couldn't acknowledge, much less speak aloud.

If they were too late to save this woman, Maggie would feel personally responsible.

"The tracks could have been here for a long time," Liz said. "Or they could be from a piece of furniture."

Maggie squatted down for a closer look. "If a lot of time passed since the marks were made, dust would have filled them in. And the trails are too wide for furniture feet but too narrow for the kind that sits on the floor."

"Oh, right. That's why you're the sleuth and not me."

Maggie walked deeper into the attic toward a rope lying on the floor. On closer inspection, Maggie saw that the ends were frayed, with a large knot between them. One section had been cut. She touched the end and a sick feeling filled the pit of her stomach. "The woman must have been tied up here."

"Do you think Chad was keeping her prisoner up here? Then he decided to sell the house and had to move her?"

"That's exactly what I'm thinking. But who is she? And where is she now?"

Liz couldn't answer.

They closed up the attic and finished their search of the upper floor. Liz looked as dejected as Maggie felt when they approached Karen in the foyer.

Maggie had only one more idea—the basement. She opened the door to reveal crumbling stone stairs.

Maggie shined her flashlight ahead and descended, apprehension settling into her stomach. She reached the packed dirt floor, and despite the light from above, sweat broke out on her palms. Maggie circled the small room with empty shelves around the perimeter, and suddenly she was back in the church cellar.

Cold. Alone. Trapped. And terrified.

Her head swam. The room blurred and began to darken as her knees went weak.

No! She wouldn't let her panic overpower her. She wouldn't faint. What if the mystery woman was still alive and feeling exactly as she had that horrible night? She spun and collided with a cold, damp wall. She righted herself and raced back up the steps to pull in deep gulps of air.

Liz shot her a look of concern. "I should never have let you go down there. Though I doubt I could have stopped you."

Too dizzy to speak, Maggie lowered her head and clasped her knees. Blood rushed back into her head, and she swayed.

"You need to sit down." Liz cupped Maggie's elbow and propelled her toward the front door, where Karen was finishing a phone call. "I hate to rush off, Karen, but Maggie's not feeling well."

"I understand."

Liz escorted Maggie outside and opened the passenger door of her car. Maggie settled into the passenger seat, shaking. Liz took her place behind the wheel and adjusted the seat.

Maggie concentrated on deep breaths until she could hold a conversation. "I can't believe how badly that cellar affected me. I knew there was nothing to be afraid of, and I still freaked out."

"The mind is a powerful thing."

"If anyone would know that, you would," Maggie said, thinking of Liz's counseling sessions.

Liz started the car and watched Maggie for a moment. "You should get something to eat."

"Why Counselor Liz, are you prescribing something sweet and delicious that can be found at The Busy Bean?"

"That's not exactly what I said." Liz glanced at her from the corner of her eye.

"Ah, but it's what I heard, and you know how powerful the mind is." Maggie winked. She was feeling better.

"Fine," Liz said. "But I'm choosing what you order."

"We'll see about that." Maggie rested her head back.

"What do you plan to do next?" Liz asked.

"You mean besides eat? I honestly don't know, but off the top of my head, I'd say I have to double my effort to find out the nurse's name. She could provide us with much-needed information. I can check at the hospital or go to the out-of-town pharmacies."

"Why don't we gather the historical society ladies together or find James and ask for advice? You know, the whole 'two heads are better than one' thing. We already have two, but more must be better."

"Sounds like a perfect idea."

By the time Liz parked in front of the coffee shop, Maggie felt like her old self, which was a good thing; she spotted James sitting at her table, and she needed her wits about her when talking to him. No telling what she might blurt out if she were addled.

"You go take a seat with James," Liz whispered. "I'll place our orders with Daisy and try to give her a reason why we rushed out of here, without telling her about the jewels."

Maggie approached the table and James stood to pull out her chair. Her knees still a little weak, she dropped onto it.

"This is becoming a habit," he said.

"A good one, I hope."

"Absolutely." He nodded at Liz. "What have you two been up to?"

"I'll tell you if you promise to keep it down. You weren't very subtle the last time I tried to tell you big news here."

He leaned closer and grinned. "You got it."

"Do you promise?"

"Yes, just tell me already!"

She gave him a detailed description of their visit to the church and the finding of the box and jewels. He held to his word and didn't speak or react except for his eyes flashing wide.

"I need you to keep this between us for now," she added.

A deep frown drew down the smile.

"Why the frown?" she asked. "I thought you'd be excited about our find."

"What if Adele was hiding the box from Chad, but he found out about it and got mad enough to kill her?"

Maggie scooted her chair closer so no one would overhear them. "Any word on the autopsy?"

"I got a call this morning. An autopsy was never performed."

"How can that be?"

"It's not uncommon when an older person is sick for a long time and the doctor signs off on the death certificate. Especially in a small town like Somerset Harbor. There was no reason to suspect foul play."

Maggie's stomach knotted. "Chad really could have killed his mother for her money and the jewels."

"Which means the stakes are now raised and we could also be dealing with murder." James pointed at her. "You need to be even more careful."

Maggie's phone rang. She looked at it more to take her mind off Chad than to see who was calling, but curiosity at the name on her screen made her answer.

"Good to hear from you, Wanda," Maggie said. "How's your father?"

Wanda Peabody sighed. "About the same. Good and bad, but he had a few moments of clarity last night and remembered Beth Thomas."

"That's wonderful! What did he say?"

"She cleared out of town, as you suspected, but she didn't go very far. Her leaving had something to do with Chad Kessler, but Dad doesn't recall the details."

Chad Kessler. Maggie resumed her suspicions about Beth's connection to the mystery. Could she have something to do with the missing chalice after all?

"Dad said she stayed in the same county," Wanda added.

"The same county? Surely someone who knew her would have run into her."

"I don't know. Dad said she kept to herself and never stepped foot back in Somerset Harbor, to keep people from learning she was still around."

"Is it too much to hope that your dad remembered Beth's forwarding address?" Maggie asked.

Amazingly, Wanda rattled it off.

"Wait, what? Say that again, please." Maggie listened carefully.

Wanda repeated the address.

"Unbelievable," Maggie said, punctuating each syllable. James was staring at her. "Did he have anything else to say about Beth?"

"No," Wanda said. "But I hope this helps."

"More than you know." Maggie thanked Wanda and hung up.

"What was that all about?" James asked.

"It's incredible. Charlie remembered Beth Thomas's forwarding address."

"And you think she's still there?"

"I know she is." Maggie could barely resist rubbing her hands together in glee over the new lead. "The address Wanda shared was for the same Beth Thomas I visited the other day."

18

Maggie drove up to Beth's house. The darkening skies threatened snow, making her wish James was with her. Liz had wanted to come, but she'd had an appointment at the church. As much as Maggie had wanted to rush off with James when he insisted on coming with her to Beth's, she felt guilty that June was still working at the antiques shop when she was so tired from the research she'd done for Maggie. Maggie had agreed to give June the afternoon off and then meet James at closing when they could drive together. But as she approached Carriage House Antiques, she changed her mind. She was so anxious to find the woman who'd been held captive for over a week that she jumped back into her car and raced to Beth Thomas's house. *I'm going to owe both James and June an apology.*

She pounded on Beth's door, letting her anger at Beth's lies strengthen her resolve to get the truth. She rattled the door and the sound rang through the nearby pines, startling birds into flight.

Beth opened the door. Her eyes narrowed when she saw Maggie.

Maggie glared at Beth. "You lied to me."

Beth crossed her arms. "Says who?"

"Charlie Frazier."

Her face paled. "You found him. I didn't think you would."

"You're a reporter. You knew it wouldn't be hard to locate him, so why tell me?"

"It just came out." She chewed her lip. "I didn't think you would pursue it."

Beth paused, and her shoulders slumped. "Or maybe I wanted someone to finally figure out what happened." Maggie took advantage of the opening.

"It involves Chad Kessler," she prompted.

Beth Thomas's defensiveness vanished and her face softened. She was ready to tell her story. "We were in love."

Maggie's mouth dropped open before she recovered. "He would've been what? Seventeen or eighteen and you—"

"Eighteen." Beth crossed her arms. "He was eighteen."

"Fine, he was eighteen," Maggie conceded.

"Yeah, I was older. People around here would have been just like you—judging us. We were going to run away together, but we needed money. So I stole the chalice from the church."

"It was you?" Maggie was shocked.

Beth's lower lip trembled as her eyes filled. "I covered Adele's last Christmas party for the paper and overheard her and Chad fighting about a special communion set that was very valuable. Because he was getting into trouble, she said she was going to hide the set to make sure he couldn't get it, and if he didn't straighten up, he'd never inherit it and she wouldn't give him his trust fund when he turned twenty-one."

"So what happened?"

"Chad had a gambling problem. He'd gotten involved with some bad people and he needed the money, so he sold the chalice." Her eyes spilled over. "And then he left me."

"That's horrible! What did you do?"

"What could I do? I couldn't stay in Somerset Harbor, so I went far enough away that I wouldn't run into people I knew, but I stayed close enough in case Chad changed his mind." She shook her head. "How pitiful is that? He dumps me and I hang around waiting."

The new facts whirled through Maggie's brain as she tried

to put all the puzzle pieces together. Finally, she settled on the first order of business. "You know I have to report you to the police, don't you?"

"Statute of limitations on the theft has long passed, so I won't have to serve time."

Maggie suspected Beth was right, but she wanted the police to sort it out. "Still, you need to go straight to the police station and report this, or I'll call them."

She gave a resigned nod. "I'll just get my things. At least this will all be in the past now, and I don't have to hide anymore. It's been awful."

"One more thing," Maggie said. "Do you know the man in the van that I saw the last time I was here?"

"No."

"So why didn't you report him?" Maggie asked, but the answer was suddenly clear. "Oh, right. You didn't want to call the police for any reason."

Beth gave an affirming nod and retreated.

Maggie waited in her car, facing the road with the doors locked and the engine running. She knew well enough that Beth might not follow through, and Maggie planned to trail her to the station to be sure she did.

Beth soon came out and drove her car down the drive. Maggie tailed her. She swung toward Somerset Harbor.

Good. It looked like Beth was really going to turn herself in. But before they reached town, Maggie's car started sputtering. She shot a quick look at the dash to check her gauges.

"No, no, no!" She hit the steering wheel. She'd been so wrapped up in the mystery that she'd forgotten to get gas. *How dumb of me. The timing couldn't be worse.*

Her car traveled a few more feet, and she managed to steer it to the shoulder before it died. She grabbed her phone and debated which friend to call. Everyone she could think of would lecture her about coming out here alone, and she was in no mood for a lecture. Better to do this on her own.

She grabbed her bag, keys, and phone, then climbed out and locked her car. The sun slunk behind gray clouds, sending the temperatures plummeting. She tugged her coat tighter around her body and trudged down the side of the snowy road. She'd walked about half a mile when a car came barreling down the road from behind her. The red Ferrari roared past her then the driver slammed on the brakes. The rear end of the car fishtailed and came to a stop. She'd seen this same car in a certain driveway in Portland.

Chad. Of all the people to drive past.

He shifted gears and backed toward her.

Had he been following her, waiting for a chance to tell her to butt out of his life? Or to kill her as he'd killed his mother? Or could he somehow have found out that she'd discovered the jewels?

Fear crept along her nerves, and she shot a look at her car to estimate the distance. No. She couldn't make it back to her vehicle before he reached her.

Time to admit she needed help. She dug out her phone and called James.

"Hey Maggie," he answered. "Don't tell me. You closed up early to go see Beth."

"Can't talk about that now. I'm a few miles outside town and I ran out of gas. Chad's here. He's getting out of his car. What should I do?"

"Keep me on the line and take a video of him. I'm on my way."

"Just the person I was looking for." He stormed toward her. "I have a bone to pick with you, lady."

She held out her phone and backed away. "I'm recording

you, and James is on the phone. If you hurt me or try to abduct me like the other woman, he'll know."

"What? Hurt or abduct you?" His anger faded to confusion as he stopped in his tracks. "Why would I do that?"

She suddenly remembered she'd never told him about the note, so she said nothing. Mentioning it would tell him she knew about the woman, and if he was the kidnapper, then he might change his mind and hurt her.

"All I want is for you to stop flapping your gums all over town about me," he continued. "Questioning my involvement in the theft of the chalice. Bringing up old stories that aren't true."

He took a step closer.

"Stop right there!" she shouted.

His feet stilled. "I can't have you dredging up all those old stories if I want the house to sell."

"I haven't said you've done anything. And I promise to stop saying you had anything to do with stealing the chalice."

"You will?"

She nodded and bit her tongue to keep from telling him about Beth's confession.

"You had better. And the other stuff you asked about," he said, much calmer now. "If I tell you the truth, you'll keep your mouth shut and stop asking questions?"

"Yes," she said though she wasn't sure she would. It all depended on his explanation.

"Fine." He shoved his hands into his pockets and looked down at his boots. "I had a bit of a gambling problem, but I finally got help. I'm embarrassed to say I had already sold off some of Mom's antiques. As she got sicker, I figured she wouldn't miss the stuff. And I was also the one who let the house go downhill. Mom didn't know how bad it was, so I figured why spend the money when I needed every penny I could get."

"You mean every penny you could steal."

He glared at her. "See, there you go again, jumping to the worst conclusion. I'm not a thief. It was only a matter of time before I got my inheritance and the things belonged to me anyway. I took them early is all."

"And the house? Yesterday you said you wouldn't sell it, but now it's for sale."

"The way you were judging me—all high and mighty like you are now—I knew you'd give me grief, so I lied about it." He raised his chin. "I don't want to sell it, but I got some estimates to repair the place and it would cost a fortune. If things aren't taken care of soon, it'll need to be torn down, and I don't want to see my family home demolished. So I had it appraised and was happy with the amount I'll get if I sell it as is."

His explanations did seem to make sense to Maggie. "There's still one thing I don't get. Without an autopsy there's no proof of how your mother died."

"Her doctor said she died of natural causes. I didn't have any reason to question that."

"Because she was old and ill, I assume he gave her a cursory look and said it was natural causes."

He scowled at Maggie. "I didn't harm my mom if that's what you're implying."

"So you wouldn't mind if an autopsy was performed on your mother now?"

He pondered her question for a moment. "I'd hate to have her exhumed, but I didn't kill her, so if the police need an autopsy to prove she died of natural causes, then I'd agree to it."

Maggie had to admit she was surprised at his willingness to have his mother's body examined, but she believed him. He had come clean about his lies from yesterday. It was looking like he wasn't guilty of murder.

He could still be holding the woman, though, and Maggie wouldn't relax until she knew he had no part in that. "There was a note in the vase I bought at the estate sale. It was from a woman claiming she was being held against her will by a man who was looking for your mother's money."

His mouth fell open, and he gaped at Maggie for a few minutes. She wanted to think his response meant he hadn't taken a woman hostage, but he could simply be shocked that the woman had been able to write a note and conceal it in the vase.

"And you believe this note?" he asked. "I mean how do you know it's not a joke or something?"

"I don't know. You tell me."

"Oh, right. I get it. You think the guy is me and I have some woman stashed somewhere. Priceless."

"Do you?" she demanded. The conversation was escalating quickly.

"Why would I be looking for her money? I inherited my mother's entire estate."

"Because your mother never told you where she hid the box with the chalice and the jewelry." Maggie's voice was harsh with the accusation.

His face showed surprise. "How'd you know about that?"

"Just an educated guess."

"Fine. So she hid a bunch of things from me. I'm already rich and don't need them."

"A gambling habit takes a lot of money. You expect me to believe you didn't want the hidden items?"

"Even if I did, I told you my gambling issues are in the past. I'd never sell them now." He took a breath. "My mom? She loved those things. I may not have made her proud when she was alive, but now I get how important those things were to her, and I would keep them."

"Until you needed more money."

He took a step toward her and clenched a fist, then suddenly let it drop. "Look. I get that I screwed up. Believe me. I know more than anyone, but I'm not the man in your stupid note."

"So who do you think wrote it and who's the man?"

His forehead scrunched up. "Tonya was the only woman besides Mom living at the house so it'd have to be her, but the guy? I have no clue."

"Tonya?" Maggie asked.

"Mom's nurse. Tonya Unger. You're not allowed to talk about her either."

At last, Maggie had the nurse's name. "Okay, but do you have Tonya's contact information so I can talk *to* her?"

Chad looked at Maggie intensely for a second, and then dropped his guard. He dug out his phone, thumbed through it, and rattled off her address in a nearby town without putting up a fight.

Thankfully, Maggie was still recording their conversation, as she wasn't sure with all the stress of the situation if she'd remember it.

"Are you happy now?" he asked. "Do you have everything you need so you'll stop bad-mouthing me?"

"I didn't bad-mouth you. I only asked questions. And I'm not going to stop asking questions until I find this woman."

Anger flared on his face, but she honestly believed his answers and no longer felt that he'd harm her.

"We're done here," he said and went back to his Ferrari.

A car raced down the road, and she soon recognized it as James's Mercedes.

Thank goodness.

She put away her phone and smiled at him as she climbed into his car. "Thank you for coming."

He didn't say a word as she settled in.

"I know, I know. I should have waited for you to go see Beth." She gave a nervous laugh. "But nothing bad happened, so it's okay." She rushed into explaining what she'd learned. "See? Now I know Beth's role in all of this and what happened to the chalice. And Chad told me the nurse's name and address."

"I know. I heard. Tonya Unger." He shot her a look. "If you're planning to go there, I'm going with you."

"Okay," she said.

"I can't go right away, though. I've been having a hard time connecting with Chad's cousin Sarah, but I just learned that she's an artist and has an exhibit tonight. I'm heading over there now. Why don't you come with me and then we can go visit Tonya together afterward."

She thought about it, then shook her head. "I'd like to go home and research Tonya on the Internet first so I'm not blindsided when we visit her."

"Sounds like a good idea, but promise you'll call me if you leave home."

"I promise."

"Let's go fill your tank and get you safely home for your research." He turned his car toward the gas station.

Maggie was antsy and couldn't relax, but her heart filled with hope.

I'm getting closer. I can still save a woman's life.

19

In the office at Sedgwick Manor, Maggie stared at Tonya Unger's social media page. It hadn't been hard to find, and Maggie could now see Tonya's posts had abruptly stopped. She had been posting two or three times per day—photos, inspirational quotes, little things that delighted or frustrated her—until a point, then nothing. Not a single posting.

Had she stopped because *she'd* been taken hostage?

Maggie had to assume that was the reason. They had to check on Tonya *now*. She dialed James and waited for the phone to ring, but she got a message that all the circuits were busy.

She tried again, with the same result.

Seriously? Is there a tower down again?

She had learned that cell service was not particularly reliable in Somerset Harbor. She couldn't wait for the cell phone company to fix the problem when Tonya's life could be hanging in the balance. Maggie would head out and keep calling James on the way. She grabbed her things, made sure she had her can of pepper spray in her bag, and then drove out of town.

Her headlights cut through a light snow drifting toward the road. If she hadn't been on a mission to check on a woman in danger, she would have enjoyed the scene the lights made through the swirling flakes. But not tonight. She tried to hurry without risking an accident in the inclement weather.

Nearly at her turnoff, she tried James's phone again and still couldn't get through. Should she wait for him when she had no idea when she'd be able to reach him? She lessened the pressure on her gas pedal.

No. Tonya could need help now.

She soon turned down a winding driveway that rambled through a thick cropping of trees. Tonya's small bungalow had crisp white paint trimmed with navy. Cute flower boxes were mounted under the front windows.

She tried James one more time, but when her call failed, she stowed her phone and strolled up the brick walk that had recently been shoveled. A light burned inside and a silhouette flickered past the front picture window. She rang the doorbell.

Loud footfalls sounded behind the door before it jerked open. A husky man in a stained T-shirt and ratty jeans glared at her from below thick brown eyebrows that grew together.

"Thought you were never coming to the door," he grumbled.

"You were expecting me?" she asked, confused.

"Nah, but we seen you sitting out there long enough. Are you coming in or what?"

He was giving off a vibe Maggie didn't like. "Is Tonya here?"

"In the living room. I'm her boyfriend, Hank."

"Can she come to the door?"

"Ah." He glanced to the side and back. His narrow lips stretched even thinner in a snide grin. "She's a bit . . . tied up right now."

She took a step back, wishing she'd thought to pull out her pepper spray before she'd left her car. "Oh, I'll come back later, then."

His eyes were ugly, and the smirk disappeared. "Now's perfect."

Before she knew what he was doing, he whipped out a gun. A very large gun.

She gasped and whirled to run.

"Oh no you don't!" He grabbed her upper arm. "You want to poke your nose into everything, do you? Want all the answers, do you? Well, I'm going to make sure you get them."

He hauled her inside, then slammed and locked the door.

Maggie's gaze darted around the small family room with worn furniture, and then quickly landed on a woman. She was petite with spiky blond hair. She was in jeans and a soiled white T-shirt that she seemed to have been wearing for some time. The scenario began to sink in. *Oh, no.* The woman was tied to a wooden dining chair with heavy ropes. Duct tape sealed her mouth and wide, terrified eyes locked on Maggie. The skin around her right eye was streaked with pale green and yellow as if she'd been struck there. But it wasn't a fresh bruise, so she had likely been a hostage for a while. *This is the note writer.*

"Tonya's been kind of lonely, haven't you, honey?" The nasty grin was back. Hank crossed the room, his solid footsteps sounding like cannon fire in Maggie's head as he approached the nurse. He dragged a chair up next to Tonya's and jerked a thumb at it. "Have a seat, nosy."

Maggie walked as slowly as she could across the room and sat as she searched for a way out of this mess.

"No sudden moves. I'm in the mood to shoot first and ask questions later." He wound ropes around her wrists and secured her upper body to the chair, then did the same thing with her ankles. He cinched the ropes tight, cutting into her flesh, but she bit her cheek so she didn't cry out and make him think she was weak. Instinct told her to struggle, but he had a gun.

If only she'd been able to get ahold of James! How she wished she'd waited until she could at least tell him where she was—or tell anyone, for that matter—so when she didn't come back tonight, someone would know where to look for her before Hank decided to kill both of them.

Kill them. That couldn't happen. She had to keep him talking to buy some time "Would you mind telling me what's going on here?" She did her best to sound calm.

He snorted. "Like you haven't figured it out."

"All I know is Tonya was Adele Kessler's nurse and you've tied her up."

He eyed Maggie. "Then why are you here?"

"I was coming to talk to Tonya to find out what she knew about—" Maggie began, but stopped short of mentioning the key in case he didn't know about it.

"No need to hold back on my account. You wanted to ask about the key and the note Tonya hid in the vase."

"She told you?"

"After a little . . . persuasion." His sneer sent a chill through Maggie. "Once she did, all I had to do was find out who bought the vase and sit back to watch you figure it out. I was surprised it took you so long."

She bit back a smart reply. It wouldn't do any good to make him angry.

Tonya whimpered again and Maggie almost joined her, but she couldn't let Hank know she was afraid of him. "How did you get involved in this?" she asked, trying to keep the fear from her voice.

"You know what? I'm getting tired of answering your questions." He ripped the tape off Tonya's mouth.

She cried out in pain. He lifted his hand and she bit down on her lip, which Maggie noticed was split and swollen. The poor girl had been through so much. Maggie's heart broke for her, and her resolve doubled. She was going to get free and make sure Hank paid for hurting a defenseless woman.

"Tonya can give you the details." He dropped onto the torn sofa, picked up a mostly empty beer bottle, and took a swig.

Great. Drunk and armed with a gun. Not a good combination.

"Tonya," Maggie said softly. "We'll get out of this. Don't worry."

"Right." Hank enjoyed that comment.

Maggie tried to ignore him. "What happened with Adele?"

"Go ahead. Spill it all," Hank growled at Tonya.

Tears formed in Tonya's eyes, but after a glance at Hank, she sniffed and took a deep breath. "It all started when I got hired to care for her. She was the sweetest person, but her son didn't want anything to do with her. Adele said it was because she kicked him out of the house when he was eighteen. She said he was a common thief and wouldn't mend his ways. It tore her up real bad. Such a shame." Tonya shook her head. "I lived with her nearly five years, and I think he only visited a handful of times."

"You lived at the house with her, then?" Maggie wanted to understand clearly.

Tonya nodded. "Hank was my boyfriend at the time, and he stayed there with me the last two years. I figured since Chad never came by, he wouldn't know about Hank. He never found out."

"Aw, come on now, honey," Hank said, smirking. "You're still my girlfriend. We get this money and we can take off together."

Maggie ignored him. "What happened to change things?"

"The last year or so, Adele lost her memory. She'd have lucid moments and then talk gibberish. On one of her good days, she said she'd hidden a jeweled key that opened a special chest with pieces for serving communion. The set had been in her family for generations and was once stored at the Kessler home. They often loaned the chalice to the church to use on special occasions, but Adele's mother had decided it was too valuable and stopped that practice. When Chad started getting into trouble, Adele worried he'd hock the set, so she hid it in the church."

"Come on, get to the good part already," Hank whined.

Tonya took a shaky breath. "The Kesslers had also hidden jewels in the false bottom of the box. Adele said she'd stashed the key in the house and that the compass would guide whoever had it to the box, but she didn't give me the location of the key or the box before she fell asleep. Trouble is, Hank overheard us talking, and he wanted to force Adele to talk." Tonya glanced at Hank and cringed. "I was often up at night with Adele, so when she napped during the day, so did I. When I was resting, Hank snuck into Adele's bedroom and threatened her."

"Yes I did." Hank stumbled to his feet and swayed. He grabbed onto a chipped wooden fireplace mantel, trying to steady himself. "Told her if she didn't tell me the location of the key and chest, I was gonna kill her." His lips curled up in a snarl. "She acted all stupid and mumbled crazy stuff. So I figured I needed to set her straight, know what I mean? So I put a pillow over her head to scare her a little. Problem is, someone can die from a pillow faster than I thought. She croaked, and I didn't even know it."

Maggie flinched and forced herself not to call him every name in the book—not only for killing poor Adele, but for being so callous and unfeeling about it.

"I saw him coming out of Adele's room," Tonya said. "He didn't have any business in there, so I ran inside. He didn't even have the decency to try to hide the pillow, just left it over her face."

"She was dead, what did she care?" he grumbled.

"Well, I cared." Tears flowed down Tonya's cheeks. "I loved her, and she didn't deserve to die."

"She wouldn't have if she'd told me where the things were." He lumbered over to Tonya.

"So he came for me, demanding I tell him where the key was." Tonya jutted out her jaw in the first hint of defiance Maggie had seen from her. "But I didn't know. He didn't believe me and said I better find it if I didn't want to end up like Adele."

"What did you do?" Maggie's voice was strained.

"At first, I tried to get help, but he pulled out that gun. Turns out he'd had it with him the whole time. He let me use my phone to call Chad to tell him Adele died, but then Hank took my phone away. I wanted to signal Chad and the people who came for Adele's body, but Hank stood right next to me and said if I talked, he'd kill me *and* the people who were just doing their jobs."

"I would've if I had to." He crossed his arms.

"How did you find the key?" Maggie asked.

"I lied to Chad," Tonya said. "Hank wanted to keep searching the house for the key so he made me tell Chad that I didn't have anywhere to go and ask to stay in the house until the estate sale."

"I take it Chad agreed."

"I kept searching for the key and finally found it in a false bottom in Adele's makeup table. When Hank was distracted, I snuck it into my pocket. I planned to give it to him, but it suddenly dawned on me. If he killed Adele, he'd kill me too if he didn't need my help to find the key. So I pretended to continue my search of the rest of the house until Hank got a call and went into the next room."

"But you couldn't follow directions, could you?" Hank's lips curled back in a jeer. "What does she do? She hides the key in the vase and writes a stupid note right under my nose."

"When it was time for the estate sale," Tonya continued, "Hank finally gave up looking for the key and dragged me here to my mother's house. She died a few years ago and left the house to me, so he knew we would be alone. Then he heard rumors in town that you had found the key, and he came home to beat the information out of me."

"We had a comfy little place to stay while Maggie here"—he thumped Maggie on the forehead—"did all the work and found the jewels."

Maggie wished she could hit him back. "What makes you think I found them?"

"You better have, little lady. If you hope to keep Tonya alive." He lifted his gun to Tonya's temple. "I don't need her anymore now that I have you. So think real carefully before you answer this question." He cocked the gun. "Where are the jewels?"

Maggie did as instructed—she thought carefully. She eyed the small family room, praying for any easy exit. Two doors led from the room, but she had no idea where they went or if the women could somehow overpower Hank and free themselves to escape. Ideas flew through her brain, fighting for attention, but most of them were foolhardy, and in the end only one thing mattered: She had to save not only Tonya's life but also her own. The only way to do that was to tell Hank where she'd hidden the jewels and hope he went to the church to retrieve the box before killing them, giving them time to try to escape.

"They're in the church," she told him, forcing the words out. "The box is in a secret door in the pulpit."

"What's a pulpit?" he asked.

"The place where the preacher stands to give his sermon."

"Okay, how do I open it?"

"Twist the trim on the right side in the middle as you're facing it."

"You telling me the truth?" He ground the barrel of the gun into Tonya's head, and she whimpered.

"I might be," Maggie said, so he wouldn't be certain and kill them on the spot instead of going to the church first. "But there's only one way to know for sure."

"Either you're a good liar, or you're telling the truth." He jerked his gun free and then shoved it in his belt. "Can't use the van since you reported it to the police, so I'll have to take your car."

Of course he's the stalker in the van.

All the pieces were fitting together now.

"Where's your phone and keys?" he demanded.

"My bag," Maggie answered, trying to shake off thoughts of this man trailing her for days.

He retrieved the tote from where she'd dropped it by the door and rummaged through it until he came up holding her keys and phone. He shoved both in his pockets. "Set your watches, ladies. Shouldn't take me more than thirty minutes to get the box and get back here." He started for the door.

"Wait," Maggie called. "What's going to happen to us once you have the jewels?"

An ugly look crossed his face. "That is one answer I don't think I have to give you."

20

Tonya started crying, but Maggie put all her attention on finding a way to escape. She searched for a sharp instrument to cut the ropes, not that she really thought she would find anything. Hank didn't seem to be the brightest bulb, but he wouldn't leave them alone with a knife lying around.

Tonya sniffled. "Thank goodness you told him where the jewels are. They are there, right?"

"Yes," Maggie said.

"Then he won't kill us."

Maggie couldn't tell Tonya that she was wrong; she needed the other woman to focus and help make their escape. Maggie kept her gaze roving the room until an idea came to mind.

"If we scoot our chairs together we might be able to untie each other," Maggie said.

"How?" Tonya asked.

"Can you pivot your chair so your back is to me?"

"I'll try." Tonya planted her feet and scooted the chair a few inches.

"That's it," Maggie encouraged. "Keep going."

Tonya bit down on her lip and put her attention on the floor as she inched closer to Maggie.

"One more bump." Tonya shoved hard. The chair caught on the corner of the rug, wobbled, then tipped over. "No!" she cried as the chair fell on its side. She landed hard and lay quietly for a moment before her tears resumed. "I should have known it wouldn't work. I've been trying to get away from Hank for days, but everything failed. Why'd I think today would be any different?" She cried harder, her chin trembling.

Maggie tried to comfort the frightened nurse. "I'm here, and there's strength in numbers. We *will* succeed."

"How?" Tonya sobbed.

"First you have to stop crying or you won't be able to focus."

"And then?"

"Then . . ." Maggie thought hard. "I'll have to tip my chair over too so you can reach my wrists. The angle will have to be just right. Hold on while I scoot my chair."

Maggie started scooting her chair inch by painful inch around Tonya. She could almost hear the clock ticking down, but she couldn't panic and make a mistake. This was their only chance. She finally reached the right place so when she tipped over she would land back to back with Tonya.

"Okay," Maggie said. "On the count of three. Are you ready?"

"Good luck," Tonya said, but her dejected tone made it clear that she didn't believe Maggie's plan would work.

"One. Two. Three." Maggie pushed off with her toes, and when the chair started to wobble, she threw her weight to the side. She crashed hard, taking the brunt of the fall on her shoulder. She stifled the cry of pain to keep from further worrying Tonya.

She took a few deep breaths to calm herself. When she could speak, she said, "Stretch out your fingers. Feel for my wrists."

Maggie extended her own hands as far as she could and felt the tip of Tonya's fingers.

"We're not close enough," Tonya said.

"I'll try to scoot toward you. You try too."

Maggie wriggled with all her might and managed to shove the chair closer. She spread out her fingers. "Yes! I have your rope."

"Thank God!"

Maggie tugged at the knot, but it didn't budge. "The knot's really tight."

"I got out of them once, so Hank's been tying them extra tight."

Doubt peppered Maggie's brain but she willed it away and focused on her fingers.

"If you hadn't figured this out, I . . ." Tonya's words fell off.

"You would have found a way to escape on your own. I can tell you're resourceful."

"Thanks," she whispered.

Maggie clawed at the rough rope with her nails. Her fingers soon ached, her nails broke, and she felt sticky blood on her fingertips, but nothing was going to stop her. She finally worked the knot loose and the rope fell free.

"You did it!" Tonya cried out. "You really did it."

"Don't celebrate yet. We still need to get the shoulder ropes." Maggie moved her chair up to give her access to Tonya's arms, then felt around until she located another knot, thanking God that Hank had tied the rope low on the chair.

"How long has he been gone do you think?" Tonya asked.

"Ten minutes," Maggie said nonchalantly, but she suspected it had been closer to twenty; they were running out of time. With new determination, she clawed hard until the knot shifted.

Tonya fidgeted, trying to loosen the upper ropes, but her efforts retightened the knot, making Maggie's job harder.

"Almost there." Maggie tried to sound cheerful instead of frustrated. "But I need you to stay still."

"I know, I just . . . I've been his prisoner for almost three weeks now. I can't be here when he gets back. I just can't." There was a sob in her voice again.

Maggie jerked the last knot free. "There. Now untie me."

Maggie felt shaking behind her back, and she suspected Tonya was crying silently. Maggie resisted the motherly urge she had to let Tonya cry it out, and gently prodded her.

"Tonya. I know this is hard. But we need to hurry."

They had perhaps five minutes left. Maggie heard Tonya's chair budge and then she felt the rope on her wrist loosen.

Thank you, God!

"I'll have you free in a minute," Tonya promised with renewed energy.

Maggie lay still. The rope shifted and fell off. Maggie twisted her wrists to get the blood flowing into her hands.

Tonya clicked her tongue. "Your fingers are bleeding."

"Small price to pay for our freedom." The rope surrounding her body loosened, and she shimmied free from it.

"Let me do your feet since your fingers are raw," Tonya said. She didn't wait for Maggie's permission but got right to work. "What happens when we're both free?" she asked as she pulled at the ropes. "Hank took our phones."

"Car keys?" Maggie asked.

"Hank has them."

"We'll have to run. How close is your nearest neighbor?"

"Almost a mile."

"We can run that far. Piece of cake, right?"

Tonya gave a reluctant nod and whisked the chair away from Maggie's body.

Maggie wiggled into a sitting position and moved her stiff feet back and forth quickly, trying to get the blood flowing.

Tonya edged closer and gave Maggie a hug. "Thank you. I couldn't have done this without you."

"You would have thought of something."

"I've been here forever. I'm pretty sure I exhausted every possibility." Tonya spun toward the door. "Did you hear that?"

"What?"

"Tires on the driveway."

Hank was back. They would have to make a run for it.

"Quick!" Maggie scrambled to her feet. "Where's the back door?"

"This way." Tonya made for the back of the room. Her steps were rigid and slow after being bound for so long.

Maggie's feet tingled, but she ignored it and placed a steadying hand under Tonya's elbow to hurry her along. Tonya groaned in pain, but Maggie kept them moving. They reached the back door, where Tonya snagged a jacket from a wall hook and slipped into it as they burst out the back door.

A car door slammed at the front of the house.

Tonya whirled, eyes wide. "He's going to catch us!"

"We need to go!" Maggie hobbled into a backyard covered in knee-deep snow. On both sides of her, she spotted large clearings, and to the back, densely wooded trees. "Into the woods," Maggie urged.

"He's going to catch up to us."

"No," Maggie said firmly. "We'll keep moving and stay ahead of him."

"But my legs are so stiff."

"I'll drag you if I have to, but we're getting out of here."

Maggie pressed Tonya through the snow and under low-hanging tree branches. They ducked deeper into the woods, where long shadows played over the pristine snow. They hadn't gone far when the unmistakable sound of the back door opening cut through the air.

"The box wasn't in the church! I won't let you get away with lying to me!" Hank bellowed.

Tonya's feet stuttered to a stop. "You lied to him?"

"No," Maggie said in confusion. "We left the jewels there. Maybe someone saw us put them back. Or maybe my friend Liz took them. She knew they were there."

She heard Hank crashing through the trees.

"Let's go!" Maggie hauled Tonya forward. With still-numb legs and feet, they couldn't outrun him, but they could outsmart him. "We have to split up. He won't know who to follow and one of us can get away to find help."

"No, I can't."

Maggie grabbed Tonya's shoulders and forced the nurse to look at her. "You can do this. Your life depends on it. Now go!" She gave Tonya a shove to the right, and after she started moving forward, Maggie ran in the opposite direction that led to the road.

She ignored the sound of Hank's footfalls coming closer, the snow that fell into her boots and chilled her feet, and the tingling that ran up and down her legs. She ran as fast as she could.

I won't stop. I can't stop.

She soon tired from lifting her legs over the snow, and trembling muscles begged her to give up. Her face and ears were numb and frozen as well. The wet snow in her boots weighed her down.

Emily's face flashed in Maggie's mind. She couldn't give up. She had to make it for her daughter.

She stumbled on and finally crested the hill. She spotted a clearing below, stopped, and shot a look around the area. Traipsing out into the open was risky.

Branches snapped behind her, and she could hear Hank grunting with effort.

Good. He'd followed her instead of Tonya, who would be no match for him. Maggie wouldn't be either, for that matter. *If he catches me.* She couldn't let that happen.

She took a deep breath and forced herself to run straight ahead. Her eyes were focused, her mind determined. She charged down the hill. The main road lay below.

I can make it there.

She glanced back and saw Hank at the top of the hill, panting, the gun in his hand. She was a sitting duck. She barreled ahead and lost her footing. Maggie tumbled into the snow and rolled, the icy coldness sliding down her back and chilling her more. She caught a glimpse of Hank moving down the hill behind her, his arm outstretched, the gun firmly held in his hand.

A gunshot sounded. A bullet cut into the snow by her head as she tumbled forward.

Fear froze her heart. There was nothing she could do.

Another bullet whizzed through the snow near her body as she tumbled farther.

She reached the bottom of the hill and landed on the shoulder of the road, her legs splayed on the asphalt. The breath was jarred from her lungs, and she lay there dazed, peering up at the gray skies.

Help me, please, she prayed. She couldn't move.

"Now I've got you." Hank was close now. He wouldn't miss at this distance.

Then she heard a car engine. She rolled to her knees to flag down the driver. She knew Hank had reached level land.

She couldn't stay here and let him shoot her. In a final great effort, she got to her feet and stumbled out into the road. The car slammed on its brakes and careened to a stop. A second car followed suit. She fled to the other side of the first vehicle and dropped behind it for safety.

Sirens suddenly blared from the car behind. A door opened.

"Drop your weapon!" a man called out. It was Officer Linton, his weapon drawn and feet planted. She was never so grateful for anything or anyone in her life.

"Drop it now!" Officer Linton called out.

Maggie couldn't see Hank, but she heard the car door open next to her. She whirled.

"James?" She blinked a few times to be sure it really was James and not some trick of her exhausted mind.

"On the ground, now!" Officer Linton was shouting. "Hands behind your back!"

James slipped out of the car and took a quick look over the hood. "You can relax. Officer Linton has the shooter on the ground."

Maggie's knees gave out, and she crumpled to the pavement.

James squatted beside her. "Are you hurt? What can I do?"

"C-cold," she managed through chattering teeth, but she suspected it was more from nerves than anything.

"C'mon. My car's nice and warm." He took her arm and helped her into the car.

She saw Hank being handcuffed, and she didn't want to think about how close she'd come to losing her life. Then she remembered the nurse, still stumbling around in the cold. When James settled behind the wheel, she begged him to take her to look for Tonya.

"We'll go," he said. "But give me a second to tell Robert so he can request a search party too." He got out to talk to Officer Linton, who had pulled Hank to his feet.

Hank caught Maggie's gaze and glared at her, hatred darkening his eyes. She jerked back. *He nearly killed me.*

She leaned into her seat and concentrated on the heavenly warmth of the car until James got behind the wheel. He handed her a bullhorn. "Robert didn't want us to leave, but I told him if I didn't take you, you'd get out and walk. I knew he carried this in his trunk and asked for it so we can call out to Tonya."

"You think of everything." She took a deep breath and gave him directions to the driveway.

"That was close, Maggie," he said when they were on the road.

"I know." She gulped. "How did you figure out where I was?" She was beginning to shiver less.

"You weren't home. It didn't take too many brain cells to realize that you'd left for some foolhardy errand on your own.

You still had Tonya's page up on your computer, so I figured that was where you'd gone."

"I tried to call. I just kept getting a message that service was unavailable. I couldn't wait. I was so worried about her. Please tell me you understand."

"I do. I don't like it, but I understand it."

"So how did you know I was in trouble?"

"I couldn't get ahold of you, and my gut said something was very wrong."

"Thank goodness for your gut." She started to smile, then thought of Tonya and clutched the bullhorn to her chest.

James stopped the car, and she jumped out and ran for the woods. She heard James follow. She put the bullhorn to her mouth and called out. "Tonya! It's Maggie! Hank's gone! He's been arrested! Come out!" There was no answer.

Maggie kept on. Fortunately, she didn't have to go far before she found Tonya lying in a heap in the snow.

"Is he r-r-really in custody?" She hugged her knees, and tears trickled down her cheeks.

Maggie nodded as James joined them. Tonya jolted back in fear.

"Don't worry," Maggie said. "This is my friend James. We'll help you to his car."

"You're safe with us," James added.

Safe. They were both safe.

Maggie exhaled a breath of relief, and the adrenaline started draining from her body. The muscles in her legs twitched, and she felt as if she might collapse, but she had to help Tonya before she could rest.

Tonya was shaking. "I couldn't run very far. I saw him go after you and I was so relieved." Her sobbing intensified. "I'm sorry. I didn't want you to get hurt, but I . . ."

"There's no need to be sorry." Maggie put an arm around Tonya and led her toward James's car. "Concentrate on the fact that you're fine. That this is all over, and Hank is going to prison for a very long time. He can't hurt you again."

"I owe you my life," she said, a weak smile forming.

At the car, James took over and settled Tonya in the backseat while Maggie sat in the front.

After James climbed in and cranked up the heat, he glanced in the rearview mirror at the woman in the backseat. "Officer Linton wanted me to tell you if we found you that we have to stay here so he can take your statement."

A new wave of concern washed over her face. "Then what? I can't stay at that house. Not after . . ."

Maggie reached back and took Tonya's hand. "You'll come stay with me until you find a permanent home. It will be nice to have someone with me. I'm a little shaken up too."

"Thank you," Tonya said as she closed her eyes.

Sirens split the quiet and flashing lights soon shone on the drive.

"It's Officer Linton." James opened his door. "I'll bring him up to speed."

Maggie couldn't let James handle everything. "Tonya, will you be okay if I go talk to the officer too?"

Tonya's response was a feeble nod before her head fell back against the seat.

Maggie climbed out, and her legs almost refused to hold her. Her feet were warming up, and they burned like fire, but she made herself walk to James and Officer Linton.

"Hank's telling a wild story about a box of jewels that you have cheated him out of," Officer Linton said.

"It's not a wild story." Maggie shared the discovery of the jewels. "Liz and I left them in the pulpit, but Hank claims they're not there."

"Where do you think they are?" Officer Linton asked.

"I don't know. Hank could have taken them and is lying about it. Or Liz could have moved them."

"I suggest you call Mrs. Young for an update while I talk with Tonya." Officer Linton walked toward James's car.

Maggie noted missed calls and a voice mail as she pressed Liz's speed dial.

Liz answered on the second ring. "Maggie. Good. I assume you got my message."

"I saw a voice mail, but I haven't listened to it."

"Then why are you calling?"

"The jewels. They're missing."

"That's the reason for my message. The janitor saw us put the box back in the pulpit. He asked me about it so I thought I should take them home with me. Not that I don't trust him, but I worried others might have seen us too."

Maggie sighed out a breath and told Liz about Tonya and Hank.

Liz was mortified. "If I'd known . . . oh my goodness . . . you or Tonya could have been killed because of me. I'm so sorry!"

"It's not your fault and I won't hear you say it is. There's no way you could have known Hank was going to come looking for the jewels. I would have done the same thing in your shoes."

"Really?"

"Really," Maggie said firmly. "Will you call Chief Cole when I get off the phone and have him meet us at your house? He can take charge of the jewels and decide the rightful owner."

"Yes. Oh Maggie, I'm so happy you're okay."

Maggie hung up and found James watching her.

"Calling Chief Cole is a good plan," he said. "I suspect when all is said and done, the jewels and communion-ware will be added to Adele's estate, which means Chad will get it."

Maggie hated that Adele's items would go to a son who'd mistreated her, but then she had no control over that. She'd located the jewels and saved a woman's life. That was all that mattered.

EPILOGUE

It was Christmas Eve, and Maggie's heart was full to bursting with joy. She linked arms with Emily and drew her closer as they strolled past the trees of the Hayward Mansion, which blazed with tiny white lights. They entered the foyer and stopped to gaze at the infamous red mercury vase, now proudly sprouting evergreen boughs, poinsettia flowers, pinecones, and a large silver bow.

Her daughter beamed at her. "The vase is perfect, Mom."

Emily pivoted on the spot, and Maggie saw the foyer through her daughter's eyes. Her eyes lingered on the fresh pine garland wound through the banister, with lovely red bows and silver balls sprinkled along its length. The overhead light reflected from the ornaments, sending bright rays through the room, as if it were alive with twinkling stars.

"It really is perfect, isn't it?" Maggie gave Emily a quick hug, and they proceeded to the parlor.

Maggie's gaze went immediately to the soaring balsam fir, covered with their handmade decorations from top to bottom. Packages wrapped in robin's-egg blue to match the fabrics around them sat under the tree with shiny silver bows. Fran had added a hand-quilted Christmas wall hanging to the far wall, and it warmed Maggie's heart to see the lovely depiction of Santa, dressed in blue and white, winking and waving with a huge sack full of toys on his back. Touches of silver and gold added sparkle to the soft blue that predominated the room. Liz stood next to the tree, greeting visitors. She caught Maggie's eye and winked. Maggie gave her a thumbs-up, but didn't interrupt.

They continued into the billiard room, where Daisy had placed a short Christmas tree on a table in the corner. Every square inch was covered with mauve ribbon, beads, and ornaments. Stockings bulging with oranges, nuts, and candy hung by the fireplace. A large wreath with silver and mauve ribbons hung above the grand fireplace. Daisy had also placed additional bows on every conceivable spot in the room. Even the velvet Louis XVI chairs didn't escape the bow-mania.

"Let me guess," Emily said, smiling. "Daisy's room."

Maggie chuckled.

The library was a far different story, but still lovely. As Liz had promised, she'd added a Limoges nativity set on the corner table. Each piece featured detailed painting and 24-karat gold embellishments, and Maggie's fingers itched to stroke them. The rest of the room was done in muted burgundy tones to match the decor, and Liz had added an authentic Saint Nicholas statue to the room as well.

Maggie checked her watch. "I don't want to be late for preservice caroling at church, so we need to pick up our pace."

They moved through the dining room, and a warm feeling lit her heart. The china from Carriage House Antiques was white with red poinsettias in the center and holly with bows ringing the outside. The pattern brightened the room and matched the red chair cushions perfectly. June had also displayed a Reed and Barton tea set with its intricate tray on the cherry sideboard and added green candles that shone from the silver.

"You all did so much work," Emily said in awe. "I had no idea it would be this grand."

"Really? Since when did you start thinking I'd do things halfway?"

"You're right." Emily grinned. "And it makes sense that you'd choose friends who think the same way."

They entered the kitchen. Ina had added a red table runner over the large island. A fresh flower arrangement with whites, reds, and greens took up the middle. An old iron candle stand held six lit white candles. She'd run greenery through a heavy pot rack above and had hung a large decorated wreath over the original stone fireplace. Maggie loved seeing the roaring fire warming even the darkest of corners.

"I can easily imagine staff preparing Christmas dinner here," Emily said.

"Be sure to tell Ina that tonight, as this was her room to decorate."

Candlelight danced in her eyes. "I'll be sure to tell everyone how amazing it is."

They were in the foyer again, and Maggie waved at Fran as they departed. She'd lock up in a few minutes and join them at the church. Maggie hustled Emily down the steps, where they paused to look at the lights again.

"Isn't this a sight?" Emily said with a contented sigh. "Just the kind of place you imagine growing up as a child."

Maggie didn't think she could feel any more joyful, but tears of happiness pricked at her eyes. How good it was to have her girl home. Maggie had devoted every possible hour to Emily since she'd arrived, making sure Emily had a special Christmas in their new home. Emily's smile and the delight in her eyes said that Maggie had succeeded.

As she climbed into the car, she reflected on her life. She was so very thankful for life, for her family, and for her friends. And tonight all of those things were wrapped up in a celebration of Christmas.

She and Emily made their way up the walk at Old Faith Chapel under stars lighting the night sky. Candles held by hundreds of worshippers lit the nativity scene as they sang in unison. Snow softly dusted the shoulders of the joyful carolers. The preservice caroling gave them a taste of the midnight service to begin in fifteen minutes.

Maggie and Emily took candles and lit them. They joined in with the group. Maggie held her candle high and sang the carol's words from her soul. When the song finished, Pastor David came forward and invited them into the service.

A sudden hush fell over the crowd. People were staring toward the sidewalk. Maggie followed their gazes to Chad Kessler, who approached on hesitant feet, the jeweled chest in his hands.

Memories of Hank and his brutal treatment of Tonya over that very chest came rushing back, and Maggie took a step back, bumping into someone. She turned to see Tonya. The nurse was clearly unnerved by the sudden jostling, and Maggie gave the jumpy girl a hug. Tonya's anxiety was improving each day thanks to Liz's careful guidance, but Tonya had a long way to go. Maggie hoped Chad's presence didn't set her back.

Chad ignored the open stares and marched up to Pastor David. Chad handed the chest over, and then raised his chin. "Open the box."

"I don't know if this is the right time," Pastor David replied quietly.

"Please. For my mother. She would want you to have it."

Pastor David cast a quick look at Maggie, who shrugged. The crowd stood silently as he seemed to struggle with himself over what to do. Finally, he lifted the lid and stared at the contents. "You found the chalice?"

"I used some of my inheritance to buy it back."

Maggie approached the men to view the communion set, together again at long last. The chalice and other serving pieces sparkled in the colorful Christmas lights strung overhead.

"I want the church to have this," Chad said.

"But it belonged to your mother, just as the jewels did," Pastor David protested, holding the chest out for Chad to take. "So it's yours now."

Chad shook his head and gently pushed the chest back to the pastor. "I want Old Faith Chapel to have it, as a testament to my mother's love for working on the altar guild." His words were choked with emotion, and he cleared his throat. "But the church can never sell it."

"We would never do that," Pastor David said. "And we will draw up a legal agreement to make sure that doesn't happen in the future." He looked at Chad with gratitude. "We will also document the history of this set. It will be good for the church to remember where it came from and what it meant to your mother and family."

Chad gave a firm nod. "I treated my mother badly over the years, and I'm sorry for that." He directed his next words to the parishioners silently watching him. "And I'm sorry for all the things I've done to the good people of this town. It took a long time for me to see how badly I behaved, but now I know I was in the wrong, and I hope you all won't hold it against me."

A buzz ran through the crowd. Maggie couldn't tell if the people were on Chad's side or against him.

"Well," he turned back to Pastor David, "I guess that's about it. I should get going so you can start your service."

He tried to leave, but Pastor David draped his free arm around Chad's shoulders. "I'd like it if you'd attend church tonight, Chad. We can use the chalice for communion."

Uneasy murmurs came from the crowd.

Pastor David released Chad and faced his flock. "Christmas is a time of hope and new beginnings. It's a time of peace and goodwill toward men. *All men.*"

Maggie took Chad's arm. *The pastor is right.*

"Welcome back to Somerset Harbor. These doors are always open to you."

He blinked at her, hardly believing what she said.

"Come on." She grasped Emily's hand and led them both up the path. She held her head high as she smiled at her fellow residents, and Emily followed suit.

Christmas Day was upon them. The day when everything was right with the world and Maggie could celebrate peace and joy with Emily and her new friends in Somerset Harbor.